BECOMING
PEACE

Kamra Smith

LUCIDBOOKS

Table of Contents

To Manville Christian Church

Chapter One

I t has taken me a while to decide where I would start my story. For many reasons, where I'm going to commence is an unfit beginning. I'll begin when I was sixteen years old, on a day that has no particular importance but is one I still remember as if it happened yesterday. I was wearing my usual brown shawl which swung over my right shoulder and fastened by my left hip. It draped over my tan cloak—a cloak that is completely unfitting and the most unflattering piece of cloth any person could design. I chose to wear brown and tan almost every day because of three reasons. One, I didn't have many other choices (it's not like I had a wardrobe or even a closet). Two, I recognized that my clothing expressed my feelings and my personality, and honestly I was a pretty dull person without much emotion and brightness for the world. Finally, reason number three: I didn't care what people thought of me.

Now, the predicament you'll find me in on this particular day is I'm playing tag. Yes, it's a childish game, I'll admit, but looking back, I find playing tag was really the only childish thing I did.

It's not as though my brother and I would plan on playing tag as often as we did. We wouldn't sit down to discuss what we'd do for the day over a hot cup of milk tea. "Yes, indeed, dear sister, I was quite hoping we would participate in a thrilling game of chase again today around noon." No, my brother and I just liked to annoy each other. He'd do ridiculous things to get me to laugh, which got me chasing after him, and I'd pester him to amuse myself, which resulted in him chasing me down. And did I mention we live in Jerusalem? There isn't much to do there when you are an unmarried female of sixteen years of age. So before you judge me, assuming this is a story of two young adults who spend their time avoiding adulthood, understand I realize this isn't the best beginning. But a story isn't really about how it begins; it is about how it ends.

I see him dash around the corner up ahead, my mother's *tzniut* flying in the wind. I try to yell insulting jokes after him about how well he resembles our aunt Marsha (neither of us is fond of her), but my rib cage is aching too much from both the run and all the laughter.

I run down the long alleys of our streets. The stone floor doesn't bother my bare feet. Mother would probably fuss at me for going barefoot, but I try not to think about that as I look down at my feet padding the dust beneath me.

Simeon jumps out from around the corner leading into the open square by the temple. "Simeon!" I laugh and begin to pull at my mother's headdress he has so terribly arranged up on his head.

Then the faint sound of an annoying pigeon coos our way. "Simeon, what are you doing?" (no, it isn't a bird, just little Miss Rebecca).

I stop clawing at Simeon's head and stand back to watch the inevitably awkward arrangement in front of me.

Rebecca is beautiful (just as her name implies). She's frail looking, like she's made of bird bones. Her feathery long brown hair is immaculately tied in a braid along her back, not a strand out of place. My brown fuzz has been in a tight bun since I woke up, but now that it is midafternoon, it hangs limp at my left shoulder. Seeing her makes me aware of the itchy feeling from the hairs on my neck. Her brown eyes perch on her head, making her beaky mouth look even more refined. She holds herself gracefully (something I've never perfected). She takes each step as if she's floating above the dirty stones beneath her.

"Hello, Rebecca," Simeon nods his goofy head her way. She blushes in response and holds her bird finger up toward his head.

"Simeon," she giggles, "Do you," giggle again, "Have you got . . ." She puts her fingers to her mouth and giggles into her hand some more. I exhale an exhausted gust of air and begin to tap my foot, feeling the dust curl up under my cloak.

Simeon laughs in response and touches his head, "Oh, this?" And he laughs some more. It seems he's forgotten about the headdress himself— no doubt dumbfounded by Rebecca's beauty.

I roll my eyes, aggravated he's playing along with this giggling charade.

"Is that a woman's headdress, Simeon?" Rebecca is able to pull her bird hand from her face and flash her dazzling smile.

"Oh, this old thing?" My brother snaps into character. "Why, it's just something I had lying around." Simeon begins to walk circles around Rebecca, his hand on his hip and the other hand flaring in the air like a prissy lady.

Rebecca roars into a fit of laughter, egging Simeon on. I can't help but smile as well.

In his most girly voice, Simeon carries on. "I was just so bored with my old tan one, you know. Today I just had to wear something to bring out the flush in my cheeks." Simeon pretends to twirl his long, non-existent hair around his index finger.

Rebecca gags with more laughter and lightly touches Simeon's arm. I feel the heat rise in my cheeks. I start to feel I'm intruding on Simeon and Rebecca's play time even though she is clearly the intruder.

"Ahem," I clear my voice as loudly as possible.

Simeon strides to my side. Staying in character, he drapes his arm over my shoulders. "Oh, Rebecca dear, you do know my dear sister, Salome, do you not?" I elbow Simeon in the rib cage as Rebecca holds her bird hand to her lips again.

Simeon is enjoying himself. One of his favorite things to do is make people laugh. One of my favorite things is to keep Simeon to myself. "Come on, you knuckle head, before all the boys in town think I have a new relative." I'd rather not have to talk to the boys in my town more than I have to. Besides, Simeon probably makes a better looking woman as an 18-year-old man than I ever would as a real girl.

Rebecca sighs as though I'm taking away her daily bread. Simeon smiles and curtly nods his head again, "Shalom, Rebecca."

Rebecca seems to have the air taken out of her as she stares at Simeon's smile. Breathlessly, she holds her two bird hands together, "Shalom, Simeon."

I roll my eyes and jerk Simeon around the corner with me, tugging his arm across my shoulder tighter around my neck. In a whispered, exasperated tone, I mock her: "Shalom, Simeon and the invisible girl you accompany."

Simeon laughs and begins to rub his knuckles on the top of my head. I feel my hair knot and frizz there. "*Sheesh*, she's annoying," I say.

"Oh, come on, Salome, be positive." Simeon starts to skip ahead of me. He is always the positive one. Everyone who knows him loves him instantly. He is always smiling and his eyes are always bright. Even when he wakes up in the morning, he's like a hyrax high on coffee beans.

It is impossible to ever get upset at Simeon. He is always happy to oblige. He, like Rebecca and every other person in the world (or so it seems to me), fits his name perfectly. He hears you, and he obeys. With this in mind, I bet you can guess who my parent's favorite is. I know they say parents aren't supposed to have favorites, but they do. It is only inevitable then, that when the un-chosen sibling discovers their ranking, they decide to play the part. I know I'm not the favorite, so I don't try to be. I don't try to please or impress my parents in the slightest. I simply am, and I think Simeon knows this.

Out of everyone in the world, he knows me best. He's good at knowing people in general because he loves to listen to others so much, but he *really* knows me. And sadly, I think he's made me a mission of his. Because he knows me so well, he knows what needs fixed and I think Simeon is a bit of a perfectionist. Now that he's had 16 years to discover all my flaws, I think he's on an expedition to find my cures.

I feel sorry for him in this regard. I'm sorry because I know what he's doing even though he thinks I have no clue. And I'm sorry because I purposely leave myself flawed so that I can keep him on an unending journey of staying close to me. I am selfish. Simeon is giving to me all the time. He's been at my side since the day I was born; a perfect older brother. And because I know every parent in this town would accept a wee clay pot in exchange for their daughter to be Simeon's wife, I selfishly remain a wreck.

As we come upon our home, Simeon pulls the *tzniut* down off his head and wads it in his fist. We exchange mischievous smiles as I lead the way inside.

The bottom floor of our house is my father's pottery shop. My father has been in business here for over 20 years. He is known in the town for his craftsmanship. I've always envied my father's talent. He's a graceful man. Rebecca could have been his daughter.

I hardly ever see the full view of my father's face. He is always hunkered down around his wheel, turning moist clay into beautiful forms. He leans close to the clay, examining it from an inch away as he smooths out every line. You can tell he loves his work. After years of spinning pots, he still observes every piece as if it only has one shot at becoming the most beautiful thing it can be. I asked him once why he looks at it so closely, so intensely. He told me, "Salome, this clay is like you and me. It only has one birth. Whoever molds it is molding it into who it will be for the rest of its life." He turned from his wheel and looked me full in the face, a rare and beautiful moment, which is probably why I remember every word he said. "I want each of my pots to like their potter." I remember being taken aback by his smile. He and Simeon have the same one.

My father glances up from his recent molding. "Hello, children. Out causing trouble again?" My father smirks to himself then bites on his tongue at the corner of his mouth as he zeroes in on an unwanted crack in his pot.

Simeon laughs, "Yes, *Abba*. Salome and I were playing dress-up in the town square." Simeon never stops walking to the ladder in the back of the room and my father only shakes his head as a smile crosses his face.

I've always appreciated my family. My parents are the most easy-going adults I've ever met. In so many ways, they are child-like. I hear my parents laugh on a daily basis (most often they are making each other laugh). My parents entertain each other. While my dad sculpts, Mother sits by his feet or on the bench in front of him and talks the whole day. I have no idea what they could possibly have to talk about all the time. They've known each other since the day they were born. How they could keep sharing new information is beyond me.

But I admire their relationship. They aren't the typical couples you see in our town. Take, for example, Beth and Eli who live next door. Eli is a fuller: he cleans old clothes to make them look new. All day you see Beth hanging up wet sheets and taking down dry ones. All day you see Beth and Eli pass each other, and all day you don't see them speak, not even look at each other. They're never mean to each other. You don't ever hear any negative words leave their mouths, but it is as if they are trying to speak to each other as little as possible. You can tell both of them are somewhat sad about their relationship, but maybe they're both too shy to do anything about it. They were probably a couple who got married because their parents were friends and Eli was probably persuaded to do so. Arranged marriages . . . I think they're secretly the death of people.

It is because of couples like Beth and Eli that I avoid any opportunities of falling in love. Even though what my parents have is amazing, it is also extraordinarily rare. It's too late for me to have my parents' story. They grew up best friends. They were like Simeon and me. They played together each and every day. They didn't have to choose to love each other. Love just happened to them.

That would be the ideal way to fall in love. You could be falling in love for years at a time but it would be growing so slowly that you wouldn't realize you were even falling. It would be a slow decline into the bubbly mass of love goop. You wouldn't feel like you were getting stuck in the mud, trapped by love's ensnarement. You would just find you had slipped into it over the past decade and now you found it quite a comfortable place to stay.

If only I were that lucky. My only choice now is to be forced into the goop.

Simeon won't have that problem. He himself is a walking puddle of love goop. His only dilemma is choosing which girl he's going to let sink into him. All the girls in town would love to have their breath taken away, slipping suddenly into Simeon's arms. But all I can say about that is, *"Good luck!"*

We were never lucky enough to get past Mother as we were with Father.

As soon as we enter the loft she's barking. "Simeon, you best have a good explanation for why you're carrying around one of my best headdresses!" Mother jerks it out of his hands and begins beating it against her thigh, watching the dust puff out.

Simeon doesn't let her swing her arms too long before he's bear-hugging her. It is no wonder he never gets in trouble. He doesn't leave enough time for consequences.

Hardly capable of breathing, Mother is still able to convince Simeon to stop swinging her about.

Mom motions for me to move into the kitchen area to begin the evening meal, forgetting all about her dusty headdress. As I knead the bread, Mother tries to make small talk with me.

"So, Salome darling, did you run into any young men while you were out today?"

Consistently for the last year, this has been my mother's topic of conversation with me. At age 16 it was high time I had settled down. My mother was 15 when she and my father had moved into their first home. To be fair to myself, it wasn't much of a home. My father had built another room onto his parent's home in Bethany. He hadn't started his own pottery business yet, so it was all he could afford. But as my mother always tells me each time she is reliving her younger years, *"We were still happy and in love."*

"No, Mother. We didn't run into boys today." Annoyed, I disguise my quick punches into the dough as though I am still kneading it.

"Well, I suppose it was for the best. By the looks of your feet, I'm assuming you were out running barefoot again, weren't you?" Mom doesn't look up from her bowl of water as she snaps the beans.

I know any other mother would have snapped into a conniption fit by now, scolding me for being such the un-marrying type. I know my mother can handle the truth though, so as I have dealt with each and every similar conversation before, I answer with great delight, "Yes, I was."

Mother sighs. I know she is trying to sound like a typical mom, exhausted with worry that her daughter will become an endless wanderer, a town laugh. But the real reason she is sighing is because she knows it isn't my fault I have become the un-marrying type; it is hers.

Her relaxed state has raised me to believe marriage isn't actually necessary, despite what every other mother is teaching her daughter these days, quite contrary to reality. Here, women are nothing but good cooks and wide hips. Here, a wife is only needed to carry on a prideful man's desire to have more of himself running around. Here, a woman has no special skill to start her own business. She is to live off the talented man. She is to be quiet and submissive, just like Beth next door. Doing and catering, filling empty stomachs and pretending God has greatly blessed her with all these to do lists and a man who enforces them.

There are times I hear the thoughts in my head and am amazed at myself. I'm impressed by my way of catching even my own being off guard. The fact of the matter is I'm a Jew. I'm *supposed* to enjoy this lifestyle. I'm *required* to endeavor to be Miss "Quiet-Pretending-to-Be-Content" Beth. And more importantly, I'm never supposed to be sarcastic with *Yahweh* God. Correction: with *Y-hweh* God. I'm not even supposed to spell his full name for I'm not holy enough. Yet, I find my brain irrationally blaspheming him.

Don't get me wrong. I love God. I love him because he created the earth so beautifully and he gave me the best big brother in the world. I love him because he led my ancestors through the Red Sea, out of Egypt, out of slavery and into the Promised Land. I love him because he has plans and he has courtesy enough to help me trust them. It's just sometimes, I don't love how it feels like I love him more than he loves me. Sometimes I think if I were God, I would enjoy my plans for myself far more than the ones he's made for me.

I think this especially when it comes to my parents. Their love story is spot-on cute, but there are chapters within it I'd deem unnecessary.

You see, my parents had two children before Simeon and me. Their names were Jude and Matthew. They were born during the reign of King Herod, the so called "Great One." My father's father passed away, leaving him an inheritance large enough to pursue his dream of opening his own pottery shop. Therefore, my parents moved to the city and began their new adventure.

They had wasted no time in procreating when they got married. My first brother, Jude—named after my father's father—was born 10 months after they had married, my mom having just turned 16 and my father being 19. A year after that, their second child, Matthew, named after my father, was born. It was then that they moved to the city, completely optimistic.

The first time my mother told me this story, I was 12, almost 13 years old. I was sitting in the cart with my mom as Dad and Simeon led the donkey back home. We were returning from Aunt Marsha's daughter's wedding in Cana of Galilee.

It was there that we met Jesus of Nazareth. Simeon and I were playing tag (yet again). I remember I had dashed under one of the tables to hide from Simeon when I heard *HIS* voice—the voice of Jesus.

His voice was sweet. It was like you could taste his words in your mouth as he said them. Each word was like a ripened grape on your tongue. I didn't see his face due to the table cloth but I imagined the most handsome man in all the land, with bright blazing eyes and lips like a full orchard. Yet as I followed his voice to match the feet I saw around the tablecloth, I registered his were among the dirtiest of the feet there. In fact, he didn't have any shoes on at all. I felt immediate affection for this man like I hadn't ever experienced before. It was as though I was at the feet of my prince and my prince was just my type, bare feet and all.

A woman had approached the table in a hustle, almost stepping on my fingers. "Jesus," she pleaded breathlessly, "they are out of wine. What are we going to do?"

I repositioned under the table, tucking in my knees so Simeon wouldn't see me. I wasn't paying much attention to the woman. I was trying to hold in my giggles so I wouldn't give away my location. But when Jesus responded, my heart stopped as I began to taste his words.

"Dear woman, why do you involve me?" He let a little laugh lapse after his words. My ear was drawn to the table top as though his lips had the tug of the Jordan undercurrent. The rest of the feet around the table stopped instantly, and I could hear men drawing slow breaths all around me as if they were expecting something. I began to anticipate something, too.

When no one said anything, Jesus broke the awkward silence. He whispered this time, "My time has not yet come."

I heard the woman set one of the wine barrels on the table. I saw her feet turn around to another pair of feet behind her. "Do whatever he tells you," she commanded as she walked away. As her feet disappeared into the crowd, I saw Simeon approaching. I braced myself for discovery as he skidded under the table.

"There you are!" He poked his finger to my collarbone. "You're it!" He started to retreat again but I grabbed at his cloak and tugged him toward me. "Wait, Simeon. Come here." He flashed his Simeon smile and scurried under like a rat. Tucking his knees like mine he glowed at me, "What are we doing?" Afraid to talk, I pointed my finger to the tabletop over our heads and held a finger to my lips, "Shhh."

Simeon's eyes followed my finger to the table top and we sat in wonder, waiting for the next drops of his words.

Jesus paced a few steps to the left then back again. He paused and I could sense he was looking at the people around him. "Please fill these jars here with water." He spoke as if he was speaking to the gentlest sets of ears in the world. As if he wanted each word he said to enter with the most tender care. Then, as if he just remembered valuable instructions, he added, "To the brim, please." All around us, the feet began to move.

Simeon looked at me as if we had just discovered a hidden treasure. I smiled in agreement, excited that he was enjoying this as much as I was.

After a while, Jesus' feet moved to the end of the table. Simeon and I watched them.

"Now, draw some out and take it to the master of the banquet." Then he added quietly, "Please." His feet were followed by many others. The table was cleared and Simeon and I dashed out to see the face of the owner of the dirty bare feet. Unfortunately, it was too crowded and the commotion only increased after he left. Everyone was in an uproar about the man named Jesus who had just turned the party's water source into the most exquisite wine.

My mother and I sit in the cart pulled by the donkey on the way home from the wedding. Simeon and Father walk ahead and I know they are talking about the same thing I want to be talking about—the man named Jesus.

"Salome, darling, did you have a good time?" Mom pulls a piece of straw from my hair I'd collected from rolling around in the cart. I knew this was my chance to find answers to my curiosity.

"Yes, Mother." I hesitate but the look on my mother's face tells me she expected me to ask exactly what I did. "Who was that man there who turned the water into wine?"

A smile spreads across my mother's face. I see excitement in her eyes as if she has been dying for me to ask. Suddenly I am annoyed at her for making me ask when she obviously wants to talk about it.

"His name is Jesus. He is from Nazareth, but he was actually born in Bethlehem, not too far from where your father and I were born." She seems proud of this. I become mildly irritated at her for throwing in a fact about herself that I already knew.

Mother is cheery now. "Some say. . ." She stops and looks deep into my eyes as if she is calculating if she should continue. After thinking for a moment she asks me, "Salome, do you recall the passage from our sacred scroll saying, *For to us a child is born, to us a son is given, and the government will be on his shoulders. And . . .*"

I know the rest of the passage. I take over for her. *"He will be called Wonderful Counselor, Mighty God, Everlasting Father, and Prince of Peace."* I look at Mom to see if she wants me to continue. She nods her head. *"Of the increase of his government and peace, there will be no end. He will reign on David's throne and over his kingdom, establishing and upholding it with justice and righteousness from that time on and forever. The zeal of the Lord Almighty will accomplish this."* Beginning to wonder if Mother is just quizzing me again, I want to stop. Luckily, the smile on her face tells me that's enough.

"Some believe that passage is about him," she says.

I become confused. "About the man at the party? Jesus?"

She nods again. "Yes. You see, that man has caused . . ." she pauses again, looking into the sky. I hadn't ever seen her think so hard before. Usually my mother spouts off whatever is on her mind without blinking an eye. I begin to comprehend this is an unusually difficult topic of conversation which explains why Simeon and Father are talking nonstop.

Mother exhales and looks down at her hands. "Salome, there is a story I need to tell you." For reasons unknown at the time, my stomach makes a flip flop.

Mother swallows hard and then sets her eyes on mine in long-term fashion. "Did you know your father and I had two sons before Simeon was born?"

Instantly, I am upset at Mother again. *Why does she have to throw such curve ball questions?* Now everything in my mind is jumbled up. *What does this have to do with Jesus and the passage about the coming Messiah?*

I shake my thoughts out of my head to try to focus on the present question. "No."

Mom glances toward Dad, and seeing he is still talking with Simeon, she turns her eyes to me again. "Well," she smiles. "We did. Their names were Jude and Matthew." Her eyes appear moist all of a sudden and she shakes her head. "Today they would be 30 and 32." She appears to juggle balls in her head. "Yes," she reassures herself, "30, and 32. Named after your grandpa and father, you know?" She smiles at me but I am too annoyed to smile back. I just want her to connect the dots. She sees my confusion and carries on. "Well, Archelaus hasn't always been king, you know?" I was only 12 but I had developed enough sense at the time to know no one lived forever. I reposition myself in the cart to show that I'm not going to answer obvious questions anymore.

Mom carries on. "Before Archelaus, his father Herod reigned." I had heard of Herod. I knew he was not a nice man.

"During Herod's reign it was rumored the Promised Messiah was coming. No one knew in what way. Many of us believed it was a great man from another land who would overthrow Herod and the entire

Roman government completely." I am delighted with this news. My ears begin to perk up, and though I don't want to allow Mom the pleasure of pleasing me so, I feel my eyes widen and I lean closer to her.

"Well, it turns out it wasn't a famous man at all." Mother smiles as if the story is still amazing her. "The Messiah came as a baby."

I suppose it made sense for the Messiah to have to be born at one point in time and all, but it was still hard to comprehend. I'd always imagined the one prophesied to save my people as a mighty warrior, not as a typical person like my dad. *No. No way.*

"There were Magi, famous Wise Men who have taught us much of what we know of the constellations today. They were certain a star in the east was the sign of the Messiah's whereabouts."

My mind recalls another passage. It scrolls through my head: *"A star shall come out of Jacob; a scepter shall rise out of Israel."*

"They followed the star and it brought them through Jerusalem. Well," Mom begins to talk faster as if the story's theme music was escalating. "The Magi started asking everyone in town where the Messiah was born." Mom shakes her head in disbelief of her own words. "Can you believe that?" she basically asks herself. I look at her as if she is going crazy. "They just came into town and started asking as if it wouldn't pose a threat at all." She stops suddenly, understanding sweeping over her face. She talks to her lap. "I suppose I would have done the same thing. I mean, I'd be pretty anxious to see the Messiah too. I don't think I could have kept quiet either." She realizes then that she has been talking to herself all the while and she appears to return to present time with me in the cart. She readjusts her cloak and continues. "Well, Herod heard of course." With this information, I knew the story could only have a bad ending.

"He requested the Magi come to him immediately. Then, because he was a dirty, sneaky snake," Mother widens her eyes and sucks her lips together, afraid that she'd said that out loud. I smile, proud of her. She sees my joy and half her lip curls into a smile as well.

"He told the Magi to find the place where the Messiah was born so he could go and worship him too." Mom rolls her eyes. "Good thing the Magi didn't believe him. I mean, who would? Herod the Great, wanting to worship a baby who would kick him off his own throne? Yeah!" The way Mom talks makes me realize where I get my sassy sarcastic sense of humor. I begin to like her more in that moment.

"So anyway," Mother sighs and begins to pick at a piece of straw in her hands. She looks weary then, old. "When the Magi didn't come back and tell him where the baby was, he made a decree that all baby boys two years and younger would be killed."

My heart begins to pound in my chest.

A single tear runs down my mother's cheek. I feel some tears beginning to brim in my own eyes. I swallow hard and tell myself I can't cry yet. I have to hear the end of the story first.

Mother peers at me from the shards of straw she's created. "Your father and I didn't have time. We didn't," she looks up into her head trying to find the answer still. "We didn't have a plan. It was just there all of a sudden." Mother looks forward at my dad. Another tear steals a path down her cheek.

"The guards were there before anyone could do anything. I heard them first at Beth and Eli's house. I heard Beth screaming for mercy. Screaming at Eli to grab their son and run." Mom's voice catches in her throat. "Their . . . their son was only a few months old. Beth had tried for so long to have a child. She thought she'd never be able to have one. Well, she was only able to have that one."

I thought of Beth next door. I saw her sorrowful face. It made so much more sense then, why Beth was always looking at the ground, never looking at Eli. It made sense then why Beth and Eli didn't talk, just worked in silence like stuffed dolls. I wondered if the last words she'd ever said to her husband were her yells for him to save their son.

"I don't want you to hate people, Salome." Mom's words catch me off guard. The images of Beth and Eli vanish and I am confused again at Mom's random word choices.

"I don't want you to hear this story and hate Roman guards. I don't want you to harbor hate for Herod or his son or anyone, okay?" I don't have words to respond. I just can't believe my mother is able to say that to me when she has every right to teach me to despise them.

"This is why I haven't told you this story before, Salome, because I see bitterness in you. You, you just get so angry with every little thing. I wanted to wait to tell you this story until I thought you would be able to forgive more easily." I quickly become offended. I am offended that Mother knows me this well. I feel my cheeks get hot but I know it isn't because of anger this time, as it usually is; it is because I am ashamed, embarrassed that my bitterness has been caught and called out.

"But after today, the person of Jesus will only make better sense if you know how the story of Jesus began." My heart suddenly seems torn. I am confused if I am to like Jesus now or not. *Was he the reason my brothers had died? Was he a bad person? How could that be? His words tasted so sweet.*

"The man at the wedding today is the Messiah." Mother looked deep in my troubled eyes. "No one has ever been such a threat in all of history. He is the reason the Magi followed the star. He's the reason a star even appeared. He came from God and God made a way for us to find him. Anyone who is against God will do all they can to make sure Jesus isn't found. They'll even kill hundreds of baby boys."

I study Mom's face. I am ready for it to crack, to see all the water of a desert burst forth. But she has an aura of peace around her. Peace that I am supposed to have—that's why she'd named me Peace. I am disappointed in myself. I know now that I want to be just like my mother.

Mother clears her throat. "Salome, do you believe any ordinary man could have done what was done at that wedding?"

I think about all the barrels of wine I had seen there. I consider *all* that water.

"No," I reply.

Mother smiles at me, "No one but the Son of God."

Chapter Two

Simeon had told me a week prior to our run-in with Birdie-Rebecca that he was going to our cousin's for a possible job opportunity. I hadn't thought much of it at the time. I think I was still distracted from our previous encounter with Josiah and his sister, Bethany. That was on Thursday. . .

Simeon and I had been on our usual path through the court square, passing time before we had to help Father make his deliveries that evening. He had been telling me of our cousin's beading business in Jericho when Bethany and Josiah started calling out to him.

This is no strange occurrence for Simeon to be beckoned while we were out walking. Daily he is approached by neighbors, strangers, and friends. I, thankfully, do not have this problem. Sometimes I find it unfortunate that Simeon does for it requires I participate in human interaction as well.

"Simeon!" Bethany prods her brother Josiah in the ribs until he catches sight of Simeon as well.

"Ah! Simeon, my friend!" Josiah is unusually similar to my brother. They are too much alike in their body shape, their wavy brown hair and dark eyes. They both have an oval face and, when they smile, dimples appear in their cheeks.

I think it was the surplus amounts of time Josiah spent with Simeon when they were younger that made Josiah's personality as cheery as my brothers. No one could be as naturally gleeful as Simeon. Josiah had to have learned it from his childhood friend.

Josiah and Simeon are as close now as they were then, though they haven't had a sleep-over in many years. Simeon has always been close to his friends though because no one needs to keep working at a relationship with him. Simeon makes them feel secure in their friendship the moment he meets them. People just trust him, desire him, and pursue to be like him.

"Hello, Joe." Simeon and Josiah embrace. "And hello, Bethany." Simeon beams his beautiful smile at her. Bethany gushes a smile. Turning redder by the second, she half hides herself behind her brother. I cross my arms and watch the rest of the people in the street scurry to and fro. I know there is no point in participating in conversation here. Bethany won't take her eyes off of Simeon the whole time anyway.

I'm not sure how long I've been staring at a stale piece of bread on the street when Simeon's jerking of my arm finally registers.

"Hmm? What?" I pull back my arm as my eyes return back into focus.

Simeon smiles at me like I am a goof. "Josiah has only been talking to you for the last minute now." Josiah and Simeon laugh simultaneously.

I become puzzled. "What?" *Why was Josiah talking to me?* "What did you say?"

Josiah's brown eyes meet my own brown eyes. "I was just trying to tell you that I like that color of shawl on you."

My eyebrows constrict. I look down at my light brown shawl. It practically disappears into the color of my hair.

"Uh, thanks Josiah." I try to sound less confused. "Your, uh, your hair looks nice."

Josiah and Simeon immediately break into laughter again. Behind Josiah, Bethany covers her lips as she giggles as well. I begin to calculate how many ways she and Rebecca are alike.

"Thanks, Salome," says Josiah. "I never thought I'd get a compliment out of you!"

Simeon laughs along and shakes his head while patting my back a few times.

"I only meant to tell you I liked it so much because it matches the color of your feet so well." Josiah pushes Simeon's shoulder as if to say,

"Wasn't that a good one?" And together they laugh some more.

Simeon wraps his arm around my shoulder. "Oh, come now, Josiah. Salome has the most beautiful feet a girl could afford. That's why she forbids covering them!"

Bethany screeches a laugh so hideous I pity her. I know instantly that if I were her I'd hide behind my brother as well.

"I only want my feet to match your hair today, Josiah." I smirk nonchalantly and let my eyes find their way back to the stale bread.

Simeon pulls me tighter to his side as he bursts into laughter. I let a smile spread across my face only because I enjoy making Simeon laugh so much.

Josiah switches weight between his feet a few times. From the corner of my eye, I see Bethany glaring at me as she wraps her fingers around Josiah's arm. I am pleased with myself.

"Well," Josiah stammers. "I can see why it is you're still single, Salome. A man could never keep a clean home with your feet." Josiah smiles at Simeon and me. He laughs only a second knowing he isn't trying to be funny anymore, but is legitimately attempting to get under my skin.

I feel Simeon steady himself, ready to respond. But I know his response is going to be boring, unoffending, and a nice byway into a pleasant goodbye, and I don't want that.

"Oh Josiah, I hadn't heard you weren't single anymore. Is there a new fad among the ladies to marry mud-heads these days?" Knowing full well that Josiah is single himself, I'm overjoyed inside at my wit.

Bethany's mouth gapes open. Josiah just gawks at me. Simeon, on the other hand, can't contain one last giggle before trying to patch up our encounter. "Nothing like good jokes among friends, eh Josiah?" Simeon pushes at his shoulder.

Josiah is able to take his eyes off me to quickly respond to Simeon, "Yeah, just joking." He looks back to me, "Right, Salome?"

I simply smile at him. I know what he wants me to say. He wants me to acknowledge my sore attitude and the fact that he is right—that I am the un-marrying type, that I have dirty feet and a boring outfit, always. I know what he wants me to do. He wants me to look away from him in shame, to blush and maybe even cry at my indecency. But I'm not that type of girl. I'm not what my name implies at all. I'm not peaceful.

Knowing I'm not going to respond, Simeon adjourns our meeting and leads me home. The way home is typical as well. I know Simeon wants to correct me, to give me pre-marital advice, but because he desires to show me he accepts and loves me more, he simply carries on with his trip plans, and I continue to half hear him.

I wake up to find *today* is the day Simeon is leaving for his trip. I throw off my sheets in a hurry.

"What? How long are you going to be gone?" I hear my attachment issues in my own voice but choose to ignore them.

"Come now, Salome. It's only a half day's walk. I'll journey back tomorrow or the day after depending on how much Micah wants to show me."

"But it's a dangerous road, Simeon!" The pleading in my voice is pathetic.

"Mom and Dad have already given me the lecture, Salome." Simeon swaddles his extra clothes and begins tying a knot at the top.

I have to beg harder if he is going to stay. "But didn't you tell me people get mugged on that road all the time?"

Simeon sighs, "I believe I told you I had heard someone saying they knew someone who got mugged on their way to Jericho *once*." He looks at me like a concerned parent. "I'll be fine."

I can tell I'm losing. Simeon is still abandoning. He is going to leave me alone with my parents for two, maybe three days, all alone. *Who am I going to walk the court with? Who is going to laugh at me when I step on rocks and yelp with pain? Who will laugh with me when I make fun of people to their faces?!*

"I'm a big boy. I can take care of myself. Don't you worry." Simeon wraps me in a hug. I squeeze him extra tight, hoping he'll feel my horror of being alone.

He pats my back letting me know the hug is over. I pull away discontented and look at my feet, not wanting him to see my puppy dog eyes. *He's right. It's only a couple of days.*

"Well, I hope you hate beading and can't wait to come home."

Simeon smiles at me. He knows a bitter remark was coming from me sooner or later.

"Yes, let's hope so. Then this treacherous journey can be all for nothing to me, but a good lesson in survival for you."

He pushes me playfully. "Then you'll have to come back and live with me forever because Lord knows I'm not going to get married with these dirty feet."

Simeon smiles but shakes his head wishing my joke wasn't true.

I beg Mom and Dad to let me walk with him at least to the Garden of Gethsemane, but they won't allow it.

"I'm not having my only daughter, of 16 years of age, walk back alone," Dad says.

"Just go find a way to occupy yourself, Salome," Mom pitches in.

So, I sit on the wall behind Beth and Eli's house watching Simeon wind his way down the streets. He stops a couple of times to see if I'm still sitting there. When he spots my pathetic-ness, he waves, smiles, and carries on.

I wish I could go with him. I hadn't spent more than 12 hours apart from Simeon since the day I was born. I remember even the nights he'd stay with Josiah, I would cry myself to sleep. Then when he'd come back the next day, I'd pretend to be mad at him for leaving. He'd spend a couple hours trying to make it up to me.

One time he even put on a puppet show for me, using some of Mom's old material. He pretended one hand was me and the other was him.

"Well hi, Salome! How are you?" The left hand says to the right.

"I'm mad! I think you smell like a big fart and look like one too!" The right hand, portraying me, says in a great impression of a girly voice.

I try not to smile then. I want the show to continue and I know as soon I appear okay again, he'll quit.

Simeon looks at me, desperate for a smile. "Oh, I guess you're right." He moves his four fingers to his thumb up and down to make it look like the material is talking. "I am a big turd."

I crack a smile. Simeon sees it from the corner of his eye and takes the play up a notch.

"Yes. Yes, you are a big turd. You know what I'm going to do with you, you big turd? I'm going to rub you all over one of my dad's clay pots and pretend you're a nasty brown glaze!"

"No, no!" Simeon cries over and over as the right arm attacks the left and beats it to a pulp. By this time I am rolling on my side with laughter. Simeon then attacks me with his hand puppets and tickles me until I am yelling for Mom and Dad to pull the big turd off me. They eventually join the fight upstairs. Mom tickles me and Dad tickles Simeon until all of us are breathless on the floor. It was a great day.

Now watching Simeon leave makes me wonder if great days like that would ever exist again. I wasn't the one who could make Mom and Dad laugh. I wasn't the one who brought our family together like that. Simeon was. It was as if he knew all the previous sorrow Mom and Dad had gone through losing Jude and Matthew and he was going to do all in his power to make up for the laughter two more sons could have brought.

Once again, the day of the wedding came back to my mind. Dad had told Simeon about our brothers long before I was told that day in the cart. When we arrive home, I ask Simeon what they had talked about, wondering if he had just found out about Jude and Matthew too.

Laying in the dark on our cots, I can see the glow of Simeon's white eyes on mine. "We talked about Jesus the whole time." Simeon smiled. "It was wonderful," he whispers.

For a moment I think I know something Simeon doesn't. "You didn't talk about how Jesus was born?"

Simeon studies me for a while. "I know about how Jesus was born. Why? Is that what you and Mom talked about?"

I am kind of jealous Simeon knew something before me. *But maybe he still doesn't know about Jude and Matthew*, I think.

"Yeah." I'm not sure how much I should say but I can't keep anything from Simeon. "Did you know—" I hesitate, then decide to jump in with both feet. "Did you know we had two other brothers before?"

Simeon rustles in the cot for a moment then props himself up on his elbow. "Yeah, I did."

I am instantly hot inside. *Why did he know and not me? Does this family like to keep secrets from me or what?!*

"Oh." I begin to turn away from Simeon but he reaches out for my shoulder.

"No, Salome. Don't be angry. I was your age when they told me too." I still am confused on why they couldn't have told us at the same time, but I choose to accept it and not stay mad at Simeon. If anything, I'll stay mad at Mom and Dad.

I turn to face him again. "Do you think that makes Jesus a bad person?"

I wish I could see Simeon's facial expressions. They usually give everything away. I wait in silence, butterflies in my stomach.

"No, Salome. Jesus was just a baby. He couldn't help it if the soldiers came into our house at that time."

I swallow in the truth. It is exactly what I want to hear.

I nod my head, but I still have a question. "Then does that make God a bad person?"

Once again Simeon is quiet but his eyes don't blink this time.

"No, Salome."

I can't tell at that moment if that is what I want to hear or not. I think I kind of want God to be the bad guy. I want someone that I can be mad at forever. Someone I can talk to, not just a random Roman soldier outside. I want someone specific.

"Remember the Exodus, Salome?" I begin to feel like a long speech is coming. If it had been from anyone else I know I would have felt immediately annoyed and have pretended to fall asleep, but I love the sound of Simeon's voice. I love how gentle he talks to me. I want a long speech from him. Those talks feel special, not like a lecture.

"Yeah," I whisper, hoping we won't wake Mom and Dad up.

"Remember how Moses led our people through the sea and Pharaoh and his guards were following and God had to collapse the water on them so our people could flee safely away from them?"

I watch the scene play through my mind and nod.

"Sometimes, bad things happen so that other people can be saved."

I wonder about that for a long moment. I think about how Jude and Matthew had to die so that Jesus could escape.

"You know," Simeon breaks through my thoughts. He is lying

on his back now, looking up at the ceiling. "Moses went through something similar."

I haven't caught on to what he is talking about yet when he continues.

"During the time of Moses, the king of Egypt hated the Hebrews. He made a decree similar to what Herod did. He said any boy born by a Hebrew woman had to be thrown into the Nile to die. And that's what happened. But remember what happened to Moses?"

"I do," I reply. "His mommy put him a basket and the Pharaoh's daughter found him."

Simeon nods his head. "Yeah, you see hundreds of babies like Jude and Matthew died so that Moses could live. And what did Moses end up doing?"

"He saved his people." Things started connecting then.

"Don't you think Jesus will do the same for his people then?"

I don't know if Simeon expects me to answer. I don't think I could. I am just taken aback, speechless. I am in wonder of God and time and how everything works out the way it does. My 12-year-old mind is blowing up inside.

"I think God has a way of working, Salome." I turn toward Simeon. His eyes are closed now. "I think something bad usually comes before something good."

Simeon falls asleep then, but I can't. I stay up hours into the night, staring at the ceiling and wondering what good Jesus is going to do for us.

Chapter Three

I try to sit on Beth and Eli's wall the whole night to display my lack of a social life without my brother to my parents but they eventually insist I come in. Truthfully, I'm kind of glad they're finally forcing me (the stones were starting to hurt my butt).

As the hours go by, I attempt to sneak out of the house to the back wall again but Mother stops me at the shop door with a ridiculous request.

"Salome, would you please take this material to Joshua's shop across town? I just love the color of the drapes he has in this front window. I don't think this material is quite the right shade but would you mind comparing them for me? I plan to make something special with it but it has to be just perfect," Mom says.

I know she is lying because sewing is not one of her favorite past times. I know she is only trying to get me out into the streets in the hopes that I bump into "some friends."

Only because I'd rather be alone in the streets than argue with Mother, I do everything she asks, including her joke of comparing material.

No sooner am I out are Mom's wishes coming true. From the corner of my eye, I see Josiah.

He picks up pace with me and begins talking as if he has been walking with me all along. I don't look at him hoping this will abash him somehow but he carries on as if he expects nothing less from me.

"Salome, it's so strange to see you out, especially without your brother. Where is he?"

I debate on ignoring him or shoving Mother's material in his face, but I'm too bored to even do that. "He's in Jericho visiting our cousin."

Josiah seems surprised, "Really? Why would he be doing that?"

I roll my eyes, still refusing to look at him so the rest of the townspeople will at least think he's talking to the wind and not to me.

"Oh, I don't know, Josiah. Why don't you go to Jericho and ask him yourself?"

Surprisingly, Josiah just laughs. "No way. You know that journey to Jericho is one of the hardest trips to make, don't you?"

I sigh, "Yes, Josiah, I know it is."

"I heard Philip's grandson was going to Jericho and he got mugged by robbers. Said two men just jumped on him when he was going around a bend in the road by some rocks. Just pounced on him like lions."

I start to feel queasy in my stomach. "Yeah, okay, Josiah. I get it."

"Where are you going?"

I can't believe it. *Why is he still talking to me? Does he not get it that I think he's appalling? Does he seriously have no other friends to bother?*

I stop and for the first time look up at him. He seems surprised that I screech to a halt so abruptly. He walks a step beyond me then jerks around, eyes wide then narrowing in on me.

I stare at him hoping he'll get the picture that I'm not going to respond and will wait for him to dismiss himself instead.

But he doesn't say anything. He only moves his lips into a little smile. It looks so much like Simeon's for a second I begin to forget that I'm mad at him.

His eyes lock onto mine then I watch them begin to look over me. He tries to do it inconspicuously, darting his eyes down to my feet, then to my eyes, then to my shoulders to my eyes, to my hair to my eyes, all really quickly.

I'm enflamed. *What, is he checking my wardrobe for more dirt, so he can make fun of me again like last time?*

I clear my throat and bug my eyes at him. "What are you doing? Trying to find another thing to make fun of me for?"

His mouth opens as if he's shocked he's been caught and his cheeks turn pink in their centers.

I'm too angry to have him continue. "I'll save you the trouble, Josiah. No, I'm not wearing shoes," I wave my left foot in the air. "And yes, I'm wearing my poopy brown shawl again that matches them. And yes, I'm single and probably will be forever because I'm dirty and I don't care. And I don't care to clean up after myself either and Lord knows a man wouldn't clean a house. No! No man is going to marry someone he'd actually have to clean for. And yes, I like being alone. I like my crappy shawl and I *don't* like you looking at me like that." Josiah's face is red and his eyes seem truthfully hurt but I don't want to acknowledge that.

"So to answer your question, Josiah, I am going somewhere you are *not* going." And with that I turn on my bare heel and head to the shop with the stupid "lovely" drapes. I don't bother to look back at Josiah even though I know he hasn't moved. I can feel his eyes watching me leave.

I feel like my shawl: poopy.

Back at home I can't stop thinking about Josiah. I think about the look on his face when I'd said all those hurtful things. I think about how I wished I had the ability to be a respectful lady like I ought to be. I wish I had kept my mouth shut for once in my life.

Truth be told, it was nice having him walk along with me. It was nice to be with someone other than my parents, rather than being alone. Someone who was so much like Simeon. I wish I hadn't made him leave me alone. Now he'll probably never bother me again. *But isn't that what I want, for Josiah to never talk to me again?*

I think about that. I picture his face in my mind. I see his short, wavy brown hair and I work my way down. His brown eyes, how they stopped to look into mine, and then how a surprising smile appeared in them. The look in his eyes confuses me. Why did they smile at me when he should have known I was going to be typical me?

I continue down. I see his small, thin nose that breaks to his thin pink lips—the lips that curl at the corners just like Simeon's when he smiles. And though they are thin, they still can hide the biggest smile behind them. That's why Simeon's smile is such a stopper. It is unbelievable that such a big smile could sneak away behind such small lips. Josiah's smile is the same way. Though I'd never looked at it full on until today, I always knew it was that way because you could see it from the corner of your eyes. It was that noticeable. Today, seeing it head on, directed toward me, I can see now how it is beautiful.

I have to stop picturing him, to stop thinking about him entirely. Doing so is increasing the guilty feeling gnawing at my stomach. I debate with myself if I should try to change who I am. *Should I try to be more quiet? More sincere? Like Bethany or Rebecca perhaps? Should I try to win the affections, the attentions, of guys like Josiah?*

I look out over Beth and Eli's wall at where Simeon had disappeared and I decide, *no, I don't want anybody but my brother back.*

This is the day Simeon is supposed to come home, day three. I have done it! I have survived two days without him. Now I only need to make it eight more hours or so until Simeon's shape appears across the city and I'll run to meet him. Until then, Mom has other plans for me.

"Salome, why don't you spend some time with your father today?"

I'm taken off guard by this. "Why? Don't you want to give me more ridiculous chores in town so I can bump into eligible bachelors?"

Mom lets her mouth hang open but I see a smile in her eyes. "Now what on earth makes you think that's what I was doing yesterday?" She smiles and folds the rag in her hands.

I just shake my head at her and make my way down stairs to Dad's shop.

He's hunched over in the corner, one eye squeezed shut, the other an inch away from the clay pot in his hands. He's smoothing out a crack I can't even see.

"Hey Dad, Mom wants me to hang out with you today." I sit on the stool next to him where my mother usually sits to stare at him while he works.

He doesn't look up at me, "Oh, is that so?" He smiles and squeezes the brim of his pot in places. I marvel at his perfectionism and wonder why I didn't get any of that in my genes.

"Well, you want to try your shot at a pot then?" Dad is smiling but I'm confused if he is serious or not.

"Me? Are you serious?" I imagine me working at a pot. The scene looks like a massacre of clay bodies.

Dad laughs and looks into my eyes, "Well sure, Salome. You're my daughter, I'm sure you've got some pot-making skills in there somewhere."

I remember the time Dad had looked me square in the face and said his pots were like his children. I couldn't believe he'd put one of their lives in my hands.

We look at each other hesitantly for a few seconds before I finally shrug my shoulders. "Don't get upset with me when people come in here thinking I've murdered your child-pots."

Dad laughs because he knows how earnestly I took him when he'd told me he was the father to all his creations.

He clears off a spot on the table beside his own wheel and sets a moist lump of clay in front of me.

"Now, Salome." Dad hunkers down so his face is level with mine. "Before you mold the clay, you have to first picture what your pitcher will look like." He giggles at his own pun. I simply smile at him, still too scared of screwing up to be as humorous as my dad is.

"After you take some time imagining, just staring at the clay, and you have the image before you, you have to lock in on it." Dad freezes in place, his eyes glazing over as if he is staring at something. "You have to keep that picture in your mind the whole time you work. It's like you won't actually be looking at the clay in front of you the whole time. You'll be looking at what it will become. That way," Dad talks faster, his excitement for his art picking up, "that way you'll know when you're done. You'll recognize the pot before you as someone you have already met." Dad wears the cheesiest smile on his face as he nods his head at me.

I know it's impossible for me to do anything he's just said because I couldn't follow half of it. He sees the distress in my face. "Salome, making pottery has to involve peace."

Yep, I think, this is definitely impossible for me.

"You can't go into this knowing you're going to mess it up. That's, that's like," he stammers for words. "That's like knowing you're going to kill it before you bring it to life."

My nerves are shot at this point.

"You are the mother, Salome. If you want a perfect baby, you have to be patient."

He nods again at me as if that surely has made a difference in my perspective.

I exhale, tired from the work already. "This is going to take a lot more brain power than arm strength, huh?" I ask.

Dad laughs and sits down at his pot. He starts smoothing his clay again, "It takes soul power, Salome."

I think that sounds kind of phony but it make sense coming from my dad. He's a very passionate man. I remember him telling Simeon and me one night at the dinner table that we had to think seriously about our career paths. I think he had been talking more directly to Simeon because I was only 11 at the time. But I still recall his words.

"Your career is more than something you do to provide for your family," he said. "Your career is just another avenue in which you are traveling to praise God. Your work should have more meaning than money. Your work should display your joy in participating in the talents God has given you." He stabbed at the lamb chop on his plate. "Remember that, you two."

I sit on my stool for a good twenty minutes trying to "picture my pitcher," before I finally begin. I see Dad smile at me from the corner of my eye as I put my hands on my clay for the first time. I immediately think of all the ways I could ruin that smile in just the next few minutes, but I desire Dad's approval today. I wish to stay out of Mom's way, too. I am set on staying in the shop as long as possible so she can't send me out to the court again where I might possibly bump into Josiah and have to deal with another dose of guilt.

No, I think, *this pot is going to be perfect. That way Mother can't bother me for not having attempted human interaction today.*

Hours pass without my knowledge. I have been sucked into my pot. I haven't even noticed that my nose is only an inch away just like my father does when he finally rouses me from dreaming.

"Salome, honey! This is looking magnificent." He arches over my shoulder gently touching the belly of my pot. I lean away from my pot and my eyes focus back into place. I study my pot as well, tracing my fingers along the smooth surface like my father. I'm surprisingly delighted as well.

I had no idea I could do something like this. Then I realize my pot is sitting sideways. It looks like an old saggy lady leaning over on an invisible cane. *Ugh! I knew I would screw this up!*

I sigh and collapse my forehead onto my hands, my elbows propped up on the table.

Dad seems surprised. "Salome, what is it?"

He has to be teasing me. *A perfectionist like himself couldn't see my slumpy grandma pot?!*

"Dad," I say looking up at him, tears in my eyes. "Don't act like you don't see that." I hold my hand up to my pot to display it. "It's all crooked. I was too close to my pot to even realize I had made it all slumped over to the left like that."

I shake my head in disappointment. Meanwhile, Dad starts to laugh.

Are you kidding me right now? Dad's going to make fun of me too? He and Josiah should be friends.

I start to get up from my stool to leave.

Dad pushes my shoulders back down. "No, don't go, Salome. I'm not laughing at you. I'm laughing because of how hard you're being on yourself."

My eyebrows constrict.

"You didn't expect this pot to just jump into your mind's picture, did you?"

I try to think about what he's saying and keep my face from blushing at the same time.

"Honey." Dad sits back down on his chair beside me, leaving me a little taller than he is. He looks up into my eyes, "A pot doesn't come as one whole piece. It comes piece by piece." Then he takes his index finger and taps it into my chest five times as he repeats himself, "P-e-a-c-e. It comes together piece by *Peace.*"

He holds his hands together in his lap, all covered in clay and he looks at me. I look at him for a while too.

"I guess what you're trying to tell me," I hold my hands together in my lap as well, "is that nothing comes easy. It takes patience. It takes time."

Dad smiles at me, glad I've caught onto his hidden message. I know his words don't come cheap. I know if he takes the time to say something, he is saying much more than what he is actually talking about.

I sigh again as Dad starts to work on his pot again. I watch him for a minute. It is the same pot he's been working on all morning. But now I see all the details within it. It is perfectly smooth in the places he wants and in other places he was using a blade to carve tiny details. Hundreds of little flower buds were springing up all around its base.

I turn back to my pot ready to spot disappointment again, only I don't. I see potential.

The day continues to pass without me realizing the existence of time. It is nearing sundown when I realize I have worked on a single pot for ten hours. Dad and I seem sucked into another world. I'd even forgotten about lunch. If it hadn't been for my mother bringing down some rice and pears I may not have eaten.

Supper was the same situation. Mother's appearance in the shop took me by surprise once more.

"Matthew, you need to teach Salome how to balance priorities." Dad and I look up from our pots in surprised confusion at Mother.

"For example," she smiles, "the importance of eating versus smoothing a pot."

Comprehension sweeps over our faces at the same time. Dad and I smile at each other. I see he is pleased with me and I'm pleased with myself for having accomplished such pleasure.

"Ah, you're right." Dad looks up at Mom smiling, then says to me, "Salome, people can live days without food so . . ." Dad isn't able to finish as Mother nudges her elbow in his ribs. The three of us break into laughter as Mom pretends to kick Dad up the ladder.

I watch them playfully disappear up the stairs while thoughts cross my mind. I think of the expression on my dad's face each time he looked at my pot. I think about my pot, and how I just succeeded at making my parents laugh without Simeon for the first time. Lastly, I think of how Simeon still isn't home.

I rush upstairs. "Mom, Dad, where is Simeon?"

The hysteria in my voice catches them off guard. After a moment of silence, Mother shrugs her shoulders. My dad looks back to me, "He may have needed to stay another day, Salome. Don't worry."

I'm instantly furious that they aren't as concerned as I am. My face burns and my mouth drops open. "But," I stammer. Mom and Dad exchange looks that say *"We knew this was coming. Yep, I told you so."*

"Did he tell you all how long he planned on being gone?"

"Yes, he said only three days but I knew he was mistaken when he told me that. It's a long, hard journey, Salome. I fully expected him to stay at least four days once he realized how hard it was just getting there, much less coming back the very next day."

I'm not given the time to respond. "Now come sit, Salome. The food is ready." Mother waves her hand at me.

Chapter Four

Another day passes without Simeon, then another. I don't feel like working on my pot anymore. I leave it to dry out. I spend most of my time on Beth and Eli's wall, just watching the road. Mom doesn't try to get me to run chores for her. She just lets me be, knowing I'm overcome with worry. Finally, on the close of day five, Mother is showing symptoms of worry too.

"Well, do you think Micah just had more for him to learn than expected?" Mother pokes at her crust of bread with one hand. She holds Father's hand with the other as we sit at the supper table.

Dad swallows the olive he is chewing and tightens his grip on her hand. "We don't have anything to worry about, Joan. Simeon is smart. I'm sure he just became more interested in the business than he expected to be."

Mother didn't seem content with the answer but looked back to her plate anyway. I assume they have probably discussed the need to stay optimistic around me with the subject of Simeon. The three of us hardly eat any of our dinner but we all pretend we are full anyway. I go to sleep with a stomach ache.

Day six is the last straw. If Simeon doesn't arrive today I'm going after him.

I sit on the wall watching the city. I stare at the bend in the road that disappears over the hill, the last stretch of Roman road I can see. I sit there through lunch. Mother doesn't bother to bring me anything like she has the days before. I know this is a sign that even she is too worried to remember to eat. The house has been quiet the past two days. All of us have wandered around, deep in thought, occasionally bumping into each other, muttering sorry and continuing with our ponderings.

A few times I see Beth looking at me from the corner of my eye. She studies my face then tries to follow my gaze over the city. Being the quiet woman she is, she never approaches me. Sometimes I wonder if it bothers her that I sit here, practically in her back yard. But, then again, I don't care.

This is technically the government's wall so I can sit here all I want.

She may want her privacy. She may think I'm intrusive. I push those thoughts away too. My brain is too crowded for them. I try to shake thoughts out. I try to imagine them falling out of my ears but my head still seems too packed. I'm exhausted even though all I've done is sit there on the wall. I'm weary from holding up a head that weighs too much with worry and fret.

I glance up at the sun to judge the time. I bet it's after three. I let my heavy head thud into my palms. I sit there with my elbows propped up on my knees, holding my face in the darkness of my hands.

"God, where is Simeon?" I pray. *"Please, I'll do anything if you could just bring him home."*

I sit there long enough to feel my arms beginning to tingle. They are falling asleep from being in the same position for so long. I'm too tired to move but I decide I feel sorry enough for my arms to put the weight of my head back on my neck.

I lift my eyes back to the bend over the hill. Nothing is there. I feel hot tears brim my eyes. As anger flashes through my body at God for the 100th unanswered prayer, I let my eyes follow the path of the road up through the city. Past the tax collector's booth the first tear falls. The second falls as I scan over two little girls playing with a stack of rocks. A third trickles down as my eyes pass a young man leading his donkey through the crowd. Attached is a cart holding dozens of young plants. From here they look like little trees. And among the trees a space has been cleared for a passenger. The man in the cart has bandages on his head and he holds a potted plant in his lap. The pot sways with the cart so I can only catch half the man's face at a time.

My eyes continue by them to a chicken flapping its wings and shaking its feathers loose of dust. Then it hits me. My tears immediately dry up by the sun as my eyes bug out of my head. I trace the road back to the man with the cart full of plants and I study the bandaged passenger.

Something in my gut is telling me it's Simeon but the potted plant keeps swaying and the large white bandage covers the other portion of his face. I'm getting more annoyed with the plant with each second when I realize the bandaged man is looking back into my eyes. Everything in me freezes as the man weakly raises his right hand. His face is showing some pain as the arm quivers, and then a familiar smile flashes across town.

I'm off the wall and running before I know what I'm doing. My body has gone into adrenaline mode. I have no recognition of the rocks that would typically make me wince and whine as they bore into my bare feet. My shoulder doesn't give in as I collide with a stranger in the street. I hear no one, stop for no one, and see only one someone: Simeon!

I nearly send the donkey into a panic attack when I collide with the cart. My arms are impulsively reaching for Simeon as the cart jerks back and forth. I hear the young man jerk on the reins, "Whoa, Nedra, whoa! It's okay girl!"

The cart hasn't quite stopped while I try to climb inside. My body seems to readjust to reality as I knock my knee against the wood. The pain enters my mind at the same time Simeon's laugh does. It's not quite the same as his old laugh. This one seems less strong, not from the gut, but riding on his breath. Nonetheless it awakens me. I see myself trying to climb into a stranger's cart, one that can't afford room for me, and I see Simeon's smile.

The cart and I stop at the same time. Simeon laughs at me and pats my hand still clinging to the cart. "Hi, Salome."

I feel more hot tears rejoin their previous position on my eye lids. "Simeon," I whisper. We smile at each other for a few moments. Only one of his eyes studies me; the other is hidden beneath a white bandage.

I grip his hand as a sick feeling enters my stomach. "What happened to you?"

Simeon's smile fades a little, remaining only as reassurance to me for what he is about to say. But before he can begin, the man who owns the cart seems to have finished calming the donkey.

He raises his voice at me as if I am a trespasser. "Hey! What do you think you're doing? Simeon, do you know this girl?"

I jerk my head around, my tears drying up again. Fully prepared to yell at whoever is interrupting my long-awaited brother, I turn then quickly shut-up.

A young man with dark olive skin stands a foot from me. He wears a serious expression that sets his square jaw in a tight manner. I can see that he iswas biting the inside of his left cheek. His round brown eyes study me as if they are calculating if I am a crazy person. And he is gorgeous.

I'm embarrassed for the first time in my life.

Simeon's weak laugh comes again. "Yes, Levi. This is my sister."

Levi's eyes study Simeon this time, determining if he is the crazy one.

Simeon waves his hand between the two of us: "Salome, Levi. Levi, Salome."

My mouth is too dry to swallow anything so I can't push down the brick in my throat in order to respond. I turn away from the beautiful-now-known-as-Levi man and stare at the pot in Simeon's lap instead.

Levi clears his throat. "Oh, well hi." He nods at me from the corner of my eye. I nod back in acknowledgement.

All is quiet for a minute. Finally a large bright smile appears on Simeon's face. "Salome, do you think you can walk alongside the cart this time instead of trying to jump in? We are on our way home."

Levi laughs as he turns to get Nedra's reins. I realize then that I still have one foot on a spindle of the wagon wheel, my arms ready to pull myself up into the cart. I manage to smile at my own stupid posture and lower myself back to the ground. *Stupid, stupid, stupid.*

I smile at Simeon. "Yeah, I can." I laugh.

Mom and Dad rush out the door of the shop at the same time. They run down the street to meet us. My mother acts as I did, going straight for Simeon's neck in a choke-hold sort of hug. My dad slows at Levi, and glancing at Simeon, he decides to let my mother strangle him some more.

"Hello, I'm Simeon's father. Who might you be?"

"Hello, I'm Levi from Samaria. I met your son on the road to Jericho. I found him nearly dead sir and I'm sorry for the long wait but the journey back with him took many days."

My father's face lightens twenty shades to a white paste. "Simeon! Son, are you okay?"

My mother releases her grip and gives Simeon a look over. "Simeon, darling, what has happened to you?" Tears are already rolling down my mother's face.

Simeon tries to move out of the cart, grunting. Levi quickly drops his reins and he and my father move to Simeon's side. "Simeon, take my hand." Levi grips Simeon's hand and places his other hand under Simeon's armpit. My father doesn't help much but makes it look like he is trying. Soon Simeon is out of the cart but he leans on Levi for support, unable to stand on his own.

"Lead me into the house, would you?" Levi nods at my dad.

Dad is stunned for a minute then jumps forward as he realizes he should indeed let this stranger in. I follow behind Simeon, Levi and my parents. I see Beth and Eli starring at us. I wonder if everyone else is as well.

Simeon is placed on his cot. Mom takes my blankets and uses them to prop Simeon further up. He looks as though he is in terrible pain and can't wait for everyone to stop touching him, so I keep my distance.

"Mom, Dad," Simeon holds his hands up as if to back them away. "I need to introduce you to a friend of mine. This is Levi." Simeon smiles proudly as if he has brought the best thing to show and tell. I would agree with him that he has.

Mom and Dad seem pleased that Simeon is still himself. "Hello, Levi," my mother nods.

"Levi saved my life," Simeon says.

My mother begins to cry again.

"Can you tell us what happened?" I think Dad is asking Simeon but Levi answers.

"I was on my way to Jerusalem from Jericho, on the same path Simeon was taking. I found him in the road. He had been beaten, probably mugged. Simeon is having a hard time remembering what exactly happened. But I've known many people who have been robbed and left for dead on that road. Well, I just couldn't leave him there." Levi turned to Simeon and they smile at each other.

My heart warms for Levi. I'm nearly overcome with gratitude. I could just kiss him right here.

"How can we ever thank you?" Mother chokes out through her tears. She pats her face with a corner of her shawl.

Levi shakes his head. "It's been a privilege getting to know your son here. Besides, I was on my way to Jerusalem anyway."

"What business do you have here?" My dad doesn't sound intrusive, only as if he is beginning to invest in Levi.

"I sell olive trees for my family."

Hence the cart full of plants.

"And your parents let you travel on that road by yourself? Why, you can't be a year older than Simeon" (a classic mother comment).

Levi smiles at her. "No, Miss. I'm only 19 years of age."

My mother shakes her head as if she can't believe it.

"But my parents are good people. They didn't want me to go either, but I have a stubborn side."

Simeon laughs, "Yes, you do!" They chuckle. Simeon turns to us, "He just wouldn't leave me be no matter how many times I asked him!" My parents laugh too. I'm too busy staring.

"Seriously though," Simeon is emotional, "Levi insisted on the best care for me. He wouldn't let me do anything for two days and he paid people to watch over me when he'd go out."

I want to fall on the floor. I want to fall at this Levi's feet and kiss them! *That's it. I'm in love and it only took ten minutes.*

"Levi, is this true?" My father seems awe-struck.

Levi doesn't blush or seem found-out in the least. "Yes. I took him to an inn along the way. I made sure he had full attention to all of his wounds. Which I should tell you," he looks at my mother, "there were many. And he had to have stitches, many bandages, and I bathed him multiple times to make sure I got all the cuts cleaned out well. But I really would recommend you bathe him tonight and make certain I got them rinsed out thoroughly." My mother nods her head in agreement. I stand amazed. I've never heard a young person talk like this before. I am in awe of his bravery, his confidence, and his total lack of any shame.

"His stitches are here," Levi points to Simeon's head above his bandaged eye, "and here." Levi shifts Simeon in the cot so he can point at a place on his upper thigh. "I think Simeon landed on a sharp rock here is how he got this cut. This injury," he motions back to Simeon's head, "was probably a rock that had been thrown at him. No doubt that's why he can't really remember what happened." Levi gives Simeon a friendly smile.

Levi clears his throat. "Simeon may have cracked ribs as well. Now I don't have a lot of experience with people, but Nedra, my donkey out there," he gestures toward the window, "she had cracked ribs before. You can feel here," Levi pushes his fingers into Simeon's side. He winces. "Right here you can feel," he takes my mother's hand and places it where his had been. "Right there something is out of place. You feel that?"

I watch my father's face to see if he has any reaction to Levi's forcefulness. He doesn't. My mother nods her head. "Yes, I feel it. Matthew, come feel." My dad moves to Simeon's side. Leaning over Levi, he gently touches Simeon's ribs.

"I'm sure you'll find out when you bathe and change him, but he's covered in bruises." My mother and father step back as Levi pushes one of Simeon's sleeves up his arm. "Here you can tell is a man's hand mark."

I try to look over Levi's shoulder to see it. Mother moves in closer blocking my view. She gasps, "Matthew, look at that! You can see four clear finger prints on his arm."

My dad looks like he is going to get sick with how pale his face is.

"I think a man must have grabbed Simeon here to pull him to the ground."

I'm seeing the whole scene in my head and I begin to understand why my dad looks queasy.

We stand around Simeon's bed for another hour or so talking about all of his wounds. Levi points out each one. Numerous times Mom bursts into tears and Dad wraps her in his arms. But Simeon is still Simeon. He smiles and laughs and, though it is weaker than it used to be, he is still alive.

When it is time for supper, we bring it to Simeon's bedside. He protests saying he can sit at the table but Mother doesn't want him to move and Levi recommends he doesn't.

"Levi, when will you be returning to Samaria?" Dad hands him some more bread.

"As I said, I was on my way to Jerusalem to sell some trees anyway. So I'll stay as long as business is good and if I run out of trees I'll have to return."

"I see. Is the tree business usually good?"

Levi sways his head back and forth. "It is enough for my family. We are not rich by any means but we have what we need and we like the business."

"Do you have other siblings?" my mother asks.

"Yes," he smiles. "I have four older brothers and three younger sisters."

"My, that is a large family. You must have a large tree farm then?"

"Yes, I suppose it's a good size. That's why my parents needed so many kids. It takes all five of us brothers to get the work done. And still, my father runs it with his brother and his sons too. My sisters even help sometimes."

I imagine myself running around with Levi's sisters through an orchard. *Paradise.*

"How old are they?" Mother continues.

"James is 30, Nehemiah is 27, Eli and Zachariah are twins; they're 23. Then there is me," his eyes meet with mine and I quickly drop them to the table. "My oldest sister, Mia is 18, Ruth is 16 and Mary is 12."

"Well isn't that fun?" I know by the look on Mom's face she is about to say something embarrassing. "You and Ruth could be friends just like Simeon and Levi are." she says to me. I simply nod my head and refuse to look at anyone.

"Ruth is almost through her betrothal year. Other than that, I'm sure she'd be a great friend to Salome."

Embarrassment: humiliation; the desire to crawl into a deep dark hole.

"Is your other sister married as well?" Mother carries the conversation.

"Mia was married at 15. Her husband helps us work the farm as well. She is pregnant now with her first child."

I know the thoughts in my family's heads are about me. I know they just have to be thinking of how Mia is 15 and Ruth is 16 and I'm 16 too, only I was the odd one. I know they're conjuring plans for me in their minds.

It really isn't fair. If Levi's sisters look anything like him it is no wonder they haven't had any trouble getting hitched.

"And how about your brothers? Are any of them married?"

Why, Mother?! Why must marriage always be on your mind?!

"Yes, all of them. I'm the one everyone is waiting on," Levi laughs. "Me and my 12 year old sister." I feel a little bit better about myself. *Wait no longer, Gorgeous Levi! I am right here. Your dreams shall come true.*

"But it's hard to fall in love when you're on the road rescuing people all the time, huh?" Simeon nudges Levi.

"I keep hoping one of these days it'll be a damsel in distress," Levi says. My family erupts into laughter but my mind is already racing with images of Levi scooping me up off the ground on the path to Jericho . . .

"Oh fair lady," he'd say. *"Why hast thou been cast down upon thy filthy ground? 'Tis as though I have discovered a rose of Sharon among the dust of this Jericho path."*

Cue wind. His hair gently blows in the breeze as he sweeps me up. Our eyes meet and he is shocked with my beauty. In that instant, he realizes his whole life has been for this very moment.

"Dear maiden, please tell me thy name."

Looking completely flawless I'd answer, "Salome."

Then he'd nearly burst into song and he'd twirl me around. "Salome, you are a rare treasure. I wish to never part from your perfection from this day on!"

And then we'd get married in the middle of his family orchard. The birds would perch in the trees and sing lovely songs through the whole ceremony. Simeon and he would embrace. "Brother," Levi would say, "You shall be my best friend for all my life. Josiah who?"

And Ruth and I would be best friends forever. We'd dance together and spend the rest of our days speaking of the love we have for our husbands.

Yes, that is the life.

Chapter Five

At night Mother bathes Simeon with Levi by her side the whole time. He instructs her on which wounds he thinks need more attention. I'm surprised that Simeon isn't ashamed by his nakedness in front of Levi. I try to imagine myself in that position but I can't get past Levi even seeing my collarbones before my heart feels like it is doing somersaults out of my chest.

I watch Levi care for Simeon and Simeon care in return. It is like Levi feels he has a responsibility to Simeon as a brother. And Simeon is so grateful. I know he must be imagining how it would have been to have Jude and Matthew there.

After the bath, Levi tries to leave to find an inn to stay at. My mother immediately refuses. She and my father insist Levi stay there at our house as long as he is in Jerusalem. I am overjoyed.

Unfortunately the bath gives Simeon a chill. He goes to bed feeling worse than when he had arrived. So with Simeon hardly sleeping, shaking with a fever to my left, and with Levi only a few feet away from me, asleep on some spare sheets to my right, I'm unable to sleep a wink. So I rise before the sun and begin to pat a wet cloth on Simeon's head.

"You look terrible." I stroke his gray cheeks.

Simeon smiles at me, "Like a big turd?"

Images of his hand puppets rush through my mind and I quietly laugh with him.

Simeon closes his eyes and drifts off to sleep. I stay there patting the cloth to his head, wiping off his cold sweat.

After starring at the white bandage on Simeon's face for who knows how long, I begin to feel eyes on me. Levi has propped himself up on his elbow, his head in his hand; laying on his side he is staring at me.

Beads of sweat form on my own head.

"That's very kind of you," Levi whispers.

I don't know what to do. I wonder if I speak if anything will come out. I take the rag from Simeon's head and pat my own, "Thanks." Levi laughs quietly then gets up from his sheets and sits by my side. Now there is sweat in my armpits and a pterodactyl comes to life in my stomach (whoever thought love was like butterflies in the tummy had apparently never seen a Levi from Samaria).

"Simeon told me a lot about you on our journey." His eyes run over my face but I can't get mine to look at him. "Oh yeah? He's really nice like that. He can talk to anybody." I try to detour the conversation away from myself (it is surprisingly modest of me).

"Yes," Levi continues. "He said you're the closest person to him—that you two are inseparable."

I smile.

"You two must be a lot alike to always be around each other." I know his statement is more of a question.

"No, Simeon is a far greater person than I'll ever be." I know I've only spoken the truth but I can't help but feel slightly sorry for myself.

"He said you'd think that."

Surprised, I look up at him. He has a pleasant smile on his face and his eyes say something more than what his mouth is, though I don't know what.

I find myself just looking at him trying to remember what was last said so I can respond. I want him to take over the conversation again to make me feel less awkward. But he doesn't. So I try, "Um . . ." The sweat is on my forehead again. Levi's smile widens at me and he shakes his head as if to say, *This girl! What is she doing?*

Then a hand touches mine. Thinking it is Levi's, I jerk my head down to find it but it is Simeon. He pushes my hand away from his face. I had the wet cloth over his lips instead of on his forehead.

Levi and I reposition so we are facing Simeon. Slowly he opens his eyes and yawns. "What are you two doing hovering over me? Don't you have something more fun to do?" He smiles and wipes at his eyes. Levi and I look at each other and smile.

Then Mom and Dad appear from behind their curtain of a wall. "Simeon," Mom starts. "How are you?"

I back away and the inspections begin. Surprisingly Levi doesn't stay with Mother to tell her what to check like I thought he would. Instead he walks toward me. Facing me he asks, "Would you like to help me sell olive trees today?"

I see Dad looking at us. I'm taken aback once again by Levi's forwardness and lack of shame. Any other man would have asked the father's permission first, if to ask anything like this at all in the first place.

I eye my dad to see what kind of response he'll give but instead he looks away.

"Sure."

After Levi explains to my parents which paths he and I will take for the day, they allow me to go with surprised looks on their faces. Simeon doesn't seem surprised, however.

"Are you sure you wouldn't rather me stay here with you?" I ask him.

Simeon laughs and rolls his eyes. "We're already going to live together forever remember? What will one day apart do?" I remember me telling him that before he left. I feel a twinge of guilt.

He places his hands on mine. "Salome, I'm fine. It's going to be a rather boring day for me. Levi could use your help. I'm sure it'll be nice to sell to people you know the names of."

The pterodactyl takes flight in my stomach again. "Okay."

I already anticipate this day will drag on with awkward silences but I put on my sandals (after looking a good while for them) and start out the door with Levi.

"Thank you so much, Salome. It'll be nice to have someone who knows the townspeople."

I nod my head. That's all I think I can do.

"This is Nedra." Levi pats the donkey's neck. "I've had her since I was five years old. She's one of my best girls, aren't you, Ned?" Levi nuzzles his nose to Nedra's. It's absolutely adorable.

"Well, are you ready to go?" Levi smiles at me.

I glance down at my feet, making certain I'd laced my sandals, then I hold my arms out at my side. "This is as good as it gets, I suppose."

Levi laughs, "I doubt that." He turns to untie Nedra while I make a little dance in my heart.

Levi wants to start on the opposite side of town from where he entered. He informs me he wants to work his way back to the path of Jericho over the bend. The walk to the other side of town alone takes an hour. To my astonishment, Levi talks the whole way.

He talks about what each of his sisters is like, what his brothers are like and their wives. He talks about his nieces and nephews and his concerns for Ruth's new marriage.

"It's not that I don't think she isn't ready to be married, I just think it all happens too fast." I soak in all his words. *I wonder if he notices that I stare at his lips.*

"Don't you think marriage is just too forced?" Levi has asked a lot of questions but none he's given adequate time for me to respond to before he carries on. This time he waits.

"Uh, yes. I guess so." I know I feel more strongly about this subject but I don't want to appear to Levi as I have to every other person in town—the un-marrying type.

"Oh come on, Salome. I know you have a stronger opinion than that. Simeon has told me."

Shocked, I begin to pick nervously at a piece of straw in my hands. "Well, fine. I think you're right. I think it's too rushed and too pressured. I mean," I feel the waterfall of my thoughts coming to shore. "I think people don't *have* to get married. It's like girls are obsessed with it. It's all my mother talks to me about." I hear the words and I stop myself. I know I could rant forever but I don't want to.

Levi laughs. "I knew it was in there somewhere." Then he wraps his arm around my shoulders and squeezes me to his side. I almost stumble over my feet as we continue to walk. My face burns from blush. The place on my arm burns from where he's touching me. The pterodactyl in my stomach freezes in mid-flap and slams to the iced over floor of my stomach.

I pull away hoping he doesn't notice I might have an allergic reaction to the male touch. "Haven't your parents arranged a marriage for you?"

Levi licks his lips that are dried from the sun. "They had, but she died." Instantly I feel like I'll puke. I was just trying to make casual conversation so he wouldn't notice how awkward I was under his arm. Now I just wished I could drape it back over me and forget the whole thing. *I'm so stupid!*

"They've arranged marriages for all of us. That's why all my siblings have married already, but me and Mary. Mary has an arranged marriage waiting for her too though. He's still alive," Levi chuckles. My eyes are still bulging from my head, shocked that he's able to carry on about this subject as if it hadn't bothered him at all that I'd mentioned it.

"Most people have arranged marriages," he continues. "Josiah explained to me why you and he don't have them: because your parents are so modern, huh?" I'm still trying to shake the fact that his betrothed is dead out of my head so I can't respond before he continues. "Your parents are really cool, Salome. You're really lucky you don't have to worry about being forced into marriage."

Lucky? Here I'd been thinking life would have been easier for me all these years if a guy was just stuck with me. Then I wouldn't have to worry about disappointing my parents or trying to win over anyone. And what did he mean by lucky? Was he glad his betrothed had died? Or was he saying I was lucky because then I didn't have to worry about my betrothed dying?

"Here we are," Levi interrupts my thoughts. "I don't guess you'll know these people all the way over here?"

I manage to shake my head no. "Right, well I'm just going to talk with them and if they want a tree it can be your job to pick one out of the cart and hand it to them, okay?" Levi smiles at me and I know then that the death must have been long enough ago that it isn't a sore spot of conversation for him. So, I nod my head in agreement and tell myself to forget the whole thing.

Levi is good with people. Not in the way Simeon is, but still good. Levi doesn't joke with them and make them feel special like Simeon would, but he can talk smart with them. He always addresses the man of the house if he is in and the men treat him as an equal.

He knows everything there is to know about olive trees. He tells them how to grow them, how to care for them, how to plant them, how to reproduce them, how to harvest the olives in all sorts of ways, and he sounds smart. The men nod their heads as Levi explains to them the importance of this investment. That planting olive trees is a lifetime benefit for generations to come. That owning an olive tree will help their family and raise the value of their land. He is a salesman. His persuasion sells a tree at nearly every other house.

Each time one is sold he motions for me to grab a plant and then he introduces me to the buyer as if they care about who I am. Every time they seem confused at Levi's introduction.

"This is Salome, a wonderful friend of mine. She's the best at choosing just the right tree for each family." Then he smiles at me and places his hand on my back as I hand the tree away.

The whole day I'm sweating, not from hard work or hot weather, but from the nervousness of knowing Levi is going to look at me again and place his hand on my back. I scold myself in all of my free time. *Stop sweating! He's going to put his hand in a puddle if you keep going like this!*

Levi never seems to notice my nerves. He only just smiles at me each time he looks at me and I think he is purposely trying to touch me as much as he can. I begin to wonder if he likes me more than just as "a wonderful friend," or if he is just this coy all the time.

When we are in view of my house, Levi takes on a slower pace.

"I had a good time with you today, Salome." He looks at my face but I still don't have the courage to look at him as much as he looks at me.

I just bob my head.

"You don't feel bad about asking me about my arranged marriage do you?" His question catches me off guard. I stop walking. I try to swallow and answer but only a steady stutter of an apology comes out.

"Look," he places his hand on my shoulder as he steps in toward my body. My nerves catch my breath in my throat. "Don't worry about that. It was a long time ago. It doesn't hurt to talk about it anymore." Relief floods my body and I'm able to pull my eyes up to his. He smiles at this. His hand begins to gently massage my shoulder. "You can ask me anything you want any time."

I swallow but it catches in my throat above the lump that has formed there. I start to choke on my spit.

Levi begins to chuckle again and shakes his head at me. He pulls his hand from my shoulder and takes a good look at me. "You don't say much, do you?"

I feel embarrassed again. *Goodness, Salome, just talk to the boy already! You've already brought up the dead-would-have-been-wife, what more do you have to lose?* But I can't think of anything to say. Finally after one last spit-loosening cough I just ask, "What do you want me to say?"

Levi smiles widely, the corners of his jaw poking out. "I want you to say you want to help me again tomorrow."

My pterodactyl springs upward, nearly into my throat. "Okay," I try to breathe. "I'd like to help you tomorrow."

All through supper Mom and Dad ask all about our journey. Levi tells them every detail they ask for. I note, however, he leaves out all the times he touched me and introduced me as his "wonderful friend." And thank God he decided not to tell them about our arranged marriages conversation. I decide not to say anything about any of it either.

"I believe Salome had a good time. I think she'd prefer to help me again tomorrow if it is okay with you." Levi doesn't look at me but at my dad. My face blushes again and I study my peas.

Dad moves uneasily in his chair but Mother seems most pleased. "Of course she can help you!" Mother chirps, "I think that it's the least we can do with how much you helped Simeon, right Matthew?"

Dad looks concerned but quickly tries to hide it. "Yes, it is."

I feel Levi's eyes on me the rest of the evening except when he is attending to Simeon's wounds. I hear them laughing together and splashing each other with the water from the sponge bath.

When Simeon and I finally have alone time, I ask how he is. "I'm feeling better than this morning," he says. "Mom's afraid that the cut on the back of my thigh has an infected stitch or two though. That's why she wouldn't let me up today. I think I'll get up tomorrow though."

I sit and listen, nodding my head.

"So," a mischievous smile appears on his face. "How was your day with *Levi*?"

I love how Simeon always knows just what I want to talk about. "It was good."

Simeon nudges me. "Come on, Salome. You can tell me all about it." I realize how blessed I am to have a brother that can fill the sandals of a sister.

"I don't know, Simeon. Do you think . . . I think . . . he may . . ." I sigh. "What would you think if I told you I think he may like me?"

Simeon sits a little straighter in his cot. "I'd ask, 'Why do you think that?'"

"Well, he introduced me to everyone. He talked to me the whole time and," I consider talking about all the touching but I hesitate too long.

"Levi is a nice guy, Salome. He's really good with people. I'm not saying he may not like you but try not to get your hopes up until he says something about it." The pterodactyl swallows a spoonful of disappointment and ceases flying.

"It's just I saw how he was with all the inn keepers." I look up at Simeon in curiosity. "I think the ladies like him. He's big for 19 years old, you know? He looks like a man, talks like a man, and," Simeon hesitates as he looks in my eyes, "and he treats the ladies as a man would."

I know Simeon is trying to tell me something but I'm not fully grasping it.

He sees my confusion. "I really like Levi. He's been like a brother to me. Makes me feel like this is how it would be if we had Jude or Matthew around." I think Simeon wants to say more but Levi enters the loft then and I excuse myself for the evening.

Chapter Six

Mother gives Simeon the okay to take occasional walks through the loft and says he can join us at the table for breakfast. But Simeon isn't allowed to do much else and insists that I make the most of the day by going outside with Levi.

Part of me is pleased Simeon gave me his blessing to travel on, but another part of me wants to just stay home. My poor stomach took such a beating the day before and I wonder if I sweat off more weight if I'll become completely boyish in figure. But we'll be approaching more of the center of town today and I'm sure I'll know more people.

The day starts just like the one before. Levi is all smiles. He wraps his arms over my shoulders and squeezes me to his side for a while. People look at us as if we are delinquent children and I'm surprised at my feeling of shame. Levi, on the other hand, doesn't stop smiling and seems to make eye contact with everyone.

The first five houses or so I don't know anyone. I'm beginning to feel like a waste of space until at last I'm able to introduce Levi to some of my dad's frequent customers. For three houses in a row I know someone and I can tell Levi is extra pleased.

And then I spot *his* house. "I don't think anyone is home there. Let's move on to the next house." I try to persuade Levi. He just shakes his head like I'm silly. "No, I think someone is home, Salome."

And before I can jerk him away from the door, Josiah is standing there.

He stops and gawks. "Salome?"

Levi looks back and forth between us.

I know I can't avoid it forever so I motion with my hand, "Levi, this is Josiah, one of *Simeon's* friends."

Levi nods his head. "How do you do Josiah? Is your father home?"

Josiah seems to ignore him. "What are you doing, Salome?"

Frustration: the feeling you get when you wish someone didn't exist in the presence of a Gorgeous-Levi-Man.

"Levi is in from Samaria. He's been staying with us and I'm helping him sell his trees."

"Olive trees," Levi corrects.

"Why is he staying with you?" I'm surprised at how Josiah can talk about Levi as if he isn't right there in front of him.

"Because *he saved Simeon*," I choose my words tactfully.

Josiah finally looks at Levi. "What do you mean *saved* Simeon?"

"He was mugged on the way to Jericho," Levi interjects. Josiah stands a half foot taller than Levi but Levi is a foot broader in the shoulders. "I found him on my way from Jericho and brought him home."

"After he took care of him at an inn for two days," I add. I feel the need to talk Levi up, to smother it in Josiah's face that he isn't the "great friend" to Simeon he thinks he is.

"Oh," Josiah glances at me then down to his feet. "Well, in that case, I'd like to help you sell your trees too." Josiah glances back at me then smiles at Levi, "As a favor to my best friend of course."

I beg in my mind, *No God! Please no!*

Levi swells in the chest like a peacock. "Yes, I see no problem in that. A friend of Simeon's is a friend of mine."

No, God! Why? Immediately sweat forms all over my face.

"No!" The word is out before I can stop myself. Levi and Josiah both look at me confused.

"I mean, if you want to help, you could just *buy* some trees."

Josiah smiles, "Nah, that won't do. I'll get my father to buy some and I'll come with you. Just wait while I get him."

I try to protest some more but Josiah is already gone. My heart beats in overdrive. *Are you kidding me? This is a worst nightmare scenario—Josiah, coming to crash on my time with a beautiful man.*

Levi turns to me as sweat runs down my forehead. "Well, he seems extra nice."

Josiah is back with his father in no time. I glare at him with a look that could kill while Levi sells two olive trees to his father. Josiah just smiles the biggest one he can at me. He is proud of himself for making me hate him on a whole new level.

As we travel on to the next house, Josiah plunges into conversation. "So Levi, the good Samaritan, huh?"

I roll my eyes as Levi smiles, "So Josiah, the best friend, huh?"

"Since we were born," he finishes. "Wish I'd have known he was hurt." He glances back at me. "How is he?"

"He's doing much better. He gave the innkeepers quite the scare when I brought him in though. He had to get 35 stitches."

"Did you see who could have done it? I mean who mugged him? Did they steal anything?"

"They took some of his clothes and his money of course. No, I didn't see who did it. He'd been laying there a good while before I found him. The blood had already dried."

Josiah seems shocked. "You don't reckon people just passed by him, do you?"

Levi shrugs his shoulders, "Wouldn't surprise me. He looked dead. I didn't know if I should stop either."

We were quiet for a minute. "Well good thing you did," Josiah finally says. He seems sincere and I stop glaring at him.

Josiah and Levi talk about their families for a long while. Levi tells him all about their olive tree business and Josiah tells him stories about him and Simeon playing around as boys. I find myself laughing at many of them.

Josiah eventually learns Levi's speech and by the end of the journey he is selling trees all on his own while Levi and I stand watching. His selling tactics are different than Levi's. He jokes with the customer and throws in personal information he knows about them. Nearly every time he gets them laughing along and they buy a tree just because they think he is such a good guy.

While he sells his last tree, Levi puts his arm around me as he has before and pulls me to his side. He runs his hand up and down my arm as if he is starting a fire there. Only the fire is starting in my head and sweat pours some more. When Josiah turns from his conversation to see us standing like that a look of confusion and anger crosses his face. Levi lets go and grabs Nedra's reins, "You ready, partner?" Levi smiles as though nothing is out of the ordinary but Josiah is looking at me differently. In fact, he hardly looks at me the rest of the way home.

When we do arrive home, I should have known Josiah wouldn't be leaving.

"Well, thank you, Josiah, for your help today." Levi wraps Nedra's reins around the post.

Josiah hardly acknowledges him, saying "You're welcome," as he disappears through the shop's front door.

The look on Levi's face is priceless. I can tell he is trying to disguise his disappointment. I think we both had wanted alone time.

We find Josiah sitting by Simeon's cot. Simeon is propped up so high he is nearly sitting all the way up.

"You look terrible," Josiah says as I enter the loft.

"That's exactly what Salome said." Simeon and Josiah laugh together.

Levi enters the loft behind me, a twinge of jealousy on his face.

"Josiah, have you met my friend Levi?" Simeon gestures toward Levi.

Josiah merely glances his way, a look of frustration beneath the surface. "Yeah, I spent the whole day with him actually."

Simeon seems surprised. "I helped him and Salome sell some trees."

"Olive trees," Levi corrects and then sits opposite of Josiah on Simeon's other side.

Josiah rolls his eyes, "Yeah, anyway, how you doing pal? Tell me what happened."

Simeon repositions. "At first I didn't remember anything. It's been coming back to me the past couple days though."

I sit on my cot behind Levi.

"I was walking along and I thought I heard something, like men talking, but I couldn't see anything. Next thing I know, something is slamming into the side of my head. Everything began spinning and I started seeing red. I guess that must have been the blood getting in my eye. I tried to keep my balance but then someone grabbed my arm and jerked me backward. All the air left me when my back hit the ground and I guess I landed on a sharp rock because," Simeon rolls slightly toward Levi and lifts his robe to show Josiah the gash on his thigh. Josiah makes a face of disgust and starts to pull Simeon's robe back down.

Simeon smiles, "I don't remember much after that. I guess they beat me up pretty good. They took my money, my shawl, my head wrap, my extra clothes, and my sandals."

Josiah shakes his head in disbelief. "How long do you think you laid there?"

Levi cut in, "It had to have been hours. When I got there, all the blood on his face had dried up from the sun."

"Yeah, when I fell backward, I saw the sun in the sky and it looked like high noon. But I couldn't tell you when Levi came because I don't remember him hauling me away or anything. I woke up in an inn with a lady over me wrapping my head."

Mother comes up the ladder into the loft. "Why shalom, everyone. I didn't know you all were home. I must have missed you coming in."

We all say hello in return. Mom dusts off her robe. "Josiah, dear! I haven't seen you in so long."

Josiah gets up and embraces her. "Hello, Joan."

I watch Levi's face as my mother and Josiah interact as mother and son. He studies them and in that moment, I am positive Levi is jealous.

"What have you been doing? Why such a long time?" Mother removes her head covering.

"I've been working outside of town at my uncle's farm." This catches me by surprise. I never pictured Josiah as responsible enough to have any kind of employment.

Mom is surprised too. "That is so great to hear, Josiah! Are you just helping him out or do you think you may pick up a trade?"

"I've been a shepherd for almost a year now. I really like it and I think I may stick with it. I might get a piece of land from my great uncle out there."

"Josiah!" Simeon bursts out. "How come you never told me? We talk nearly every day."

Josiah turns slightly pink in his cheeks. "It's nothing."

"Yeah right, nothing! That's really cool, man. Isn't it, Levi?" Simeon nudges him and Levi wears a pained smile, "Yes. The world will always need shepherds."

Josiah seems hurt by his comment. Even I start to feel a nudge of annoyance with Levi. I understand that Josiah is a pain in the butt, but strangers have no reason to be rude to him, especially if he has just helped them sell a dozen trees. *Correction,* I hear myself think, *olive trees.* I laugh inside at myself.

"Josiah, you must stay for supper," Mom insists. "You have to tell Matthew about all your adventures outside the city. I think he really misses farming sometimes. We haven't been out of town in so long."

Josiah nods his head, agreeing he'll stay. Usually I think I would have broken down by this point. I probably would have whined like a baby at Mom for having invited Josiah to stay, but today I'm kind of curious. There is bound to be entertainment with Levi and Josiah in the same room.

Chapter Seven

Simeon is able to sit at the table for the first time. He sits at the far end, looking much like my dad who sits at the opposite end of the table. I sit next to Simeon by my mother and directly in front of me is Josiah and to his side, Levi. I am pleased with the arrangement. At this spot I can watch both of their faces.

Unfortunately, dinner starts as expected. Mother brags about Josiah's secret shepherding skills and my father asks a billion questions about his uncle's land (supposedly, my father and Josiah's uncle were old friends). Next, is *more* trivia about Josiah's great uncle's land. Everyone but Levi seems impressed by Josiah's desire to move out of the city. I even find myself kind of impressed. I mean, Josiah never came across as anything but a city boy to me. *Maybe there is more to him than I thought.*

"It surprised me too. I always thought I'd just buy another shop in the city and take up a trade like you and my dad did," Josiah nods to my father. I try to picture Josiah as a tent-maker, like his father, or as a potter, like my dad. When I do, I discover it is actually pretty hard to see him doing one of those things. The more I think about it, the more it makes sense that Josiah should be a shepherd. He's gentle and patient. Anyone who works with stupid sheep all day would have to be.

My dad nods his head back, "A lot of things aren't as they appear to be." Josiah bobs in agreement. I wonder if Dad is reading my mind.

By this time, I've finished my supper ten minutes ago. Everyone else has been more disciplined and is taking their time poking their food around to prolong dinner conversation.

To pass the time, I study the differences between Josiah and Levi. I note how Levi sits with perfect posture. He sits with a spare cloth in his lap and he wipes off his fingers after each bite. He doesn't look up much at anyone. I think this is only because Josiah is here.

Josiah doesn't seem to notice Levi at all. He slouches like I do over top his plate so he'll drop the food back on the table instead of his lap. He's already gone through two glasses of water and is nearly finishing the third. He mostly talks to my father, keeping respectful eye contact but in between bites he looks over to me and then to Simeon.

We are all surprised when Levi finally does say something. "I think tomorrow will be my last day here. I don't have many trees left and I need to get back in time to celebrate the Passover with my people."

He didn't say "my people" in any way in specific but it still catches me off guard. The whole time he's been here I haven't thought about how Levi is a Samaritan. I've been too caught up in thinking how handsome his face is to register anything else.

All at once, thousands of thoughts rush through my mind. *I couldn't marry Levi. My people would disown me. Why hasn't anyone said anything yet about Levi? They must not know he's a Samaritan. Would they have bought trees from him if they knew? Is that why he introduced me as his friend? So people would think he was from around here? But does it really matter that he's from Samaria? What is so bad about it anyway? I mean besides the fact that they worship on the wrong mountain and don't observe all the scrolls that we do. What really is the problem? Levi has seemed nice enough. He doesn't seem like a half-breed barbarian to me.*

Mother's high pitched voice interrupts my thoughts. "Would you be leaving tomorrow or staying another night?"

"I think I'll just leave tomorrow. I can't thank you enough for letting me stay as long as I have."

Mother waves her hand. "It hasn't been long at all. It doesn't seem long *enough* actually for all that you did for Simeon."

Levi swells in the chest again. He is glad *he* is finally getting attention.

"Oh, it was nothing really." Levi smiles broadly. I think back to the first day he was here and how he never denied his good work. Now, his words seem too much like Josiah's, as if he is trying to prove he is the better man. Maybe I won't be sad that Levi is leaving.

"It was a pleasure getting another great friend." Levi acknowledges Simeon at the end of the table.

He smiles in return but I notice he doesn't seem sad to hear Levi is leaving either, or else he would have insisted he stay at least one more night. Instead he says, "I'll be forever grateful."

Before an awkward silence can occur, Mom joins in: "You're right, Levi. It is nearly Passover. Before long, we'll need to purge the house." Mother is talking more to herself than anyone else, as if she were making a mental list of what to do.

Dad shakes his head. "I have a good feeling about this year. I think we can anticipate something good, something different this year."

Simeon suddenly beams with delight, "Maybe we'll see Jesus in the city."

Suddenly anticipation grows in my stomach. Everyone at the table seems more awakened—except for Levi.

"I've heard of him," Levi nods his head at Simeon. The rest of us are confused. When no one says anything, Levi gets the idea and continues. "There was a woman in my village who met him."

He looks around the table at us. We stare at him, eager to hear the story. When no one continues to say anything, Levi clears his throat. "Well she isn't the most credible source in my book." He laughs a little but none of us join because we haven't the slightest clue what he is talking about. He catches the drift.

"She's been the town prostitute for longer than I've been alive." He has judgment in his tone. "She's been married five times." He looks around at us for some sign of shock but we are still bewildered.

"No one in the town has ever liked her because of, well, you know . . . because of her lifestyle. So, she always went to the well in the middle of the afternoon, the hottest part of the day, because she knew no one else would be there." He shakes his head as if he doesn't believe the story himself.

"She came running back into town one day—it was last year, last summer, I think. She came yelling she'd met a man named Jesus at the well and he told her all about her life even though she'd never laid eyes on him before. Said he was the greatest prophet she'd ever met. She said he had eyes like fire, whatever that means. But anyway, she got the whole town worked up. A bunch of people ran out to the well to see if he was still there but of course he wasn't. But that didn't stop them. Everyone in the whole town started to believe Jesus was this great prophet. They said he was the Messiah."

Smiles appear on all of our faces. We all glance around the table at each other, acknowledging the smiles and nodding that we all agree with this statement. Levi seems taken aback.

"I take it you guys believe the same thing?"

"Yes, we do," my dad says quietly (not to be secretive, but to keep the mood of peace that had settled around us). "At least I can speak for my family. I don't know about Josiah." Dad glances toward him and, for the first time, Levi turns to look at Josiah too.

I hadn't thought about Josiah believing in Jesus. I realized that I never cared to know before. Tonight feels different. I hold my breath hoping Josiah is going to agree with us.

Josiah turns to Simeon and they smile at each other as if they know something we don't. Then Josiah turns back to my father. "I also believe Jesus is the Messiah."

We all smile again but Levi. His eyebrows have constricted. He was the most perplexed person in the world at this moment. He shakes his head trying to understand.

"Did you not believe the woman?" my dad finally asks.

I already know the answer. "Well, I did at first. I mean, we all got caught up in it. She was so . . ." he looks at the ceiling for the word, "different I guess. Different from what she had been. She looked different if that makes sense. She was happy and it was the first time I'd ever seen her talk to people in the open before. She wasn't embarrassed or shy. She was just shouting and jumping. That's . . ." He shakes his head, "I guess you'd just have to know her, the before and after her, to understand what I'm saying."

"No, I think I can imagine it," Dad interrupts.

Levi just nods his head, disappointed with the direction the table talk has gone. This isn't the attention he wanted. "I believed her at first. I went to the well about every day for the next six weeks to see if he'd come back." I swallow a mouthful of sadness for Levi as I picture him running through the barrenness of Samaria to a well in the heat of the day. "He never showed and I guess it's kind of faded. I realize it could be true but I'm not like her and I'll probably never be, all running around from town to town constantly talking about him."

More sadness: sadness tastes gross when you're not used to it. It must be like milk tea. You have to acquire the taste for it.

"In a way you kind of are like her," Dad observes as he breaks the silence. Levi looked like he was straddling a fence, prepared to fall over in offense. "You're always traveling from town to town, aren't you?" Dad smiles. I know then that he is trying to move the conversation into a more comfortable zone for Levi. It works. Levi rolls his shoulders back and sticks his peacock chest back out.

"Yes, that is true." His bragging voice is back. "I couldn't imagine standing around in one place all day like you shepherds."

Another jab at Josiah? If someone doesn't say something to him, I'm going to.

Luckily, Simeon speaks before me. "Shepherds don't stand around much, do they Josiah? I mean you're always moving the herds aren't you?"

"Yeah, I mean it depends on the day. You've got to take your herds where the land isn't run down. You have a rotation. And sheep are always getting into trouble. You've got to get them out of thistles, always round them up at night or they'll wander off. But in general, yeah," Josiah turns and smiles at Levi. "Shepherds do get a lot of down time."

A cocky smile doesn't appear on Levi's face with the recognition he is right. He looks defeated. I am just blown away by the Josiah in front of me tonight. It's like I don't know him at all.

The rest of the evening takes a more casual tone. Dad eventually stops badgering Josiah with farming questions and he and Mother fall into their own conversation. Josiah and Simeon take off in their own world as well, only this time I don't mind standing there listening in. I don't even care that Levi is left looking like a sour olive on his makeshift cot.

When it is time for Josiah to go, I find myself wishing there were more hours for our evening. I wish he could take Levi's place in the cot not far from mine. I think I just might enjoy seeing his smiling face more than Levi's too-high-and-mighty-yet-ever-so-perfectly-construct-ed-man-face.

Josiah walks Simeon back to his cot after Mother announces she thinks it is time he rests.

"Thanks for coming over today, Josiah. I've missed you. I'm sorry I can't walk you out, perhaps you can, Salome?"

I drop my sheet from my cot to the floor.

"No, Salome doesn't want to walk me to the door, Simeon." Josiah laughs and pulls a sheet up over Simeon's legs.

"And why wouldn't I want to?" I jerk my sheet back up off the floor.

Josiah turns to me, a bit of surprise and suspense in his eyes. "Because you don't like mud-heads, remember?"

I feel myself smile inside. "Yeah, I don't. That's why it would be my honor to see you out as soon as possible."

The smiles on Josiah's and Simeon's faces are priceless. Behind me, I can feel Levi's eyes boring a hole into my back. I hear him wrestle in his sheets louder than necessary, probably trying to get me to look at him, but I don't. I make a bee line for the ladder in the floor and hear Simeon quickly whisper after a hustling Josiah, "Bye pal."

Knowing it will appear too polite, I don't cross the threshold but hold the door wide open for Josiah.

He crosses my path into the street and turns to look at me. The moon light brightens the right side of his face, making a white crescent appear in his brown eye. It is mesmerizing and I can't look away.

"I didn't know it was in you to be so tolerable, Salome."

I sigh, "Yes, well my patience has worn out now, Josiah, so . . ." I wave my free hand as if telling him to move on down the street. Inside, I really want him to stay and hope he finds a way to make the conversation longer while we play through our charade.

He changes weight to his other foot and leans against the door frame. The moonlight lessens on his face and I realize how much in the dark we are.

Josiah sighs, "Ah, when will I ever get on your good side, Salome?"

I roll my eyes. "The day I have one, Josiah."

"So, never?" He smiles.

I laugh but try to cover it up with a fake cough, "Yes, never."

Josiah laughs and pushes himself from the door frame. My heart skips. *Oh, don't go.*

Josiah looks at his feet and passes some dirt between them. "See me tomorrow, will you, Salome?" He turns his eyes back to mine, the crescent reappearing.

I try to think if I have heard him correctly. "Why?"

As soon as I say it I know it sounds more rude than I want to play so I try to fix it. "I mean, why when we don't have any more trees to sell?"

"Olive trees." He corrects me. We exchange a knowing smile.

"I only thought I'd let you feel I was giving you a choice because I'll be here tomorrow whether you want me to or not to see Simeon. That is unless you're leaving with Levi?" Josiah shyly darts his eyes away from me.

Layered with sarcasm, I reply, "And risk the chance of never seeing you again? Now why would I even consider that?"

Though we are in the darkness, I would guarantee Josiah turned pink. He laughs, "Yes, there's really nothing appealing about that option is there?"

A chicken clucks its way down the street. It makes me realize how quiet the city is. *It's late.* My arm is getting stiff from holding the door and I let it close further.

Josiah shuffles back a step into the street. "Alright, well." I realize he's taken my stiff arm as a sign that I want him to go. I push it all the way open again.

"I have to go to Madam Rosalyn's tomorrow to pick up some more bandages for Simeon, if you want to go with me." The words leave my mouth so quickly I'm not sure if they are even true. I wonder if Simeon will need more bandages and, if he doesn't, what kind of scheme will I have to come up with to make it true.

Josiah looks like a little school boy as he turns on his toe toward the street. Smiling, he nods his head. "I told you I'd see you tomorrow."

Chapter Eight

I can hardly sleep and this time it isn't because Simeon is on my mind, and it isn't even the fact that the breathless-at-first-sight-Levi is sleeping a few feet from me. I can't sleep because Josiah's smile keeps playing through my mind. It is as if my mind has a repeat button for a ten-second clip of Josiah turning on his toe, his boyish face lit up like the moon.

My stomach rolls even when I'm trying my best to lay still. I can hear Levi huff and puff occasionally when I won't stop flopping around in my sheets. I'm too giddy to sleep. I can't believe I am thinking of Josiah this way. I can't believe I thought the boy who annoyed me so much all my life is now the most adorable creature.

A thought brings my eyes wide open. *Simeon. Would he be upset or happy that I liked Josiah? Would it ruin their friendship? How do boys work anyway? Do they want to become brothers-in-law or is that breaking some kind of guy code?*

I have to stop thinking about it before it ruins my good mood. I should sleep, but by now I can catch a glimpse of dawn approaching.

Mother woke up shortly after I dozed off because no sooner had I fallen asleep when the smell of breakfast began wafting through the air.

Mom has prepared a great feast for the morning meal, an unusual practice, but I know it is because it is Levi's last day.

Levi is packed when I wake up. He must be as eager to leave as I am to see him go.

Simeon is even out of bed and assisting Mom in setting the table by the time I have finished rubbing my eyes. I know it is going to be a great day before I even stretch my way out of bed.

"Mother, I would like to walk with Levi to the city gate today."

Mother looks petrified at Simeon's words. "I don't know if you're well enough for that, dear."

Dad shakes his head. "If you're up for it Simeon, get out of here. You need some fresh air. You've been cooped up in this loft for days now."

Mother perches her lips and flicks at the crumbs on her plate.

"I'll go with them to make sure Simeon can get back, Mom."

"Thank you, Salome. I was going to suggest that." Mom picks up her plate and takes it to the water bowl.

Dad winks at me then turns to Levi. "Levi, Joan and I would like to buy some of your trees if you have the availability. It is the least we can do for all that you have done for my son."

Levi wipes his mouth with his cloth. "You are welcome to as many trees as you like, Matthew."

Dad smiles, "We'll take three then. I do hope you get back safely, Levi. We'll have to come across each other again soon so I know you're well."

"I'll have to come visit you," Simeon adds. I hear Mother drop her plate.

Levi laughs, "I think I want to see you looking more *alive* next time, Simeon. You better stay off the Jericho path. *I'll come to you.*" The rest of us laugh as well and, before I know it, Levi's cart is loaded aside from three *olive* trees that he sits aside, outside the shop door.

Dad spends some time saying goodbye and repeating multiple times safety precautions Levi should take along the way. Mom keeps wrapping her arms around him, hugging around his waist because she is much shorter than he is, and telling him repeatedly to wish his family the best.

I'm pleased I won't be meeting them after all.

While Mom and Dad repeat their (again), Josiah shows up. Mother is then wrapping her arms around him too.

"I came to play with Simeon today, but what is this? You're out?!" Josiah and Simeon embrace.

"I'm free," Simeon jokes. "I get to walk the other prisoner to the gate today."

Mother starts to rant about how she thinks Simeon shouldn't be leaving the house and the difference in opinion she and Matthew share about what healthy looks like, "and what prison looks like for that matter," she concludes.

Josiah makes his way toward me eventually.

"I'm walking with him and Levi to the gate," I explain before he asks.

"Ah, then I will assist you." Josiah smiles and turns on his toe again. "Simeon, my lad, maybe you should ride in the cart down there and *then* walk home."

Levi looks aggravated with Josiah's suggestion, probably because he'll have to rearrange his cart again or maybe because he didn't think of it first.

"I'll be fine," Simeon protests.

"Don't be stupid." Josiah begins pushing olive trees around. Levi huffs, drops Nedra's reins and nudges Josiah out of the way. "I'll get it."

Josiah looks pleased with himself. "Thanks, Levi. How thoughtful of you."

Levi rolls his eyes and I am so pleased Josiah is here to provide me with adequate entertainment.

Once at the gate, Levi and Josiah help Simeon out of the cart (it looks like a game of tug-of-war between them more than assisting a handicapped victim). Without haste, Josiah slaps Levi on the back and says, "Have a nice trip home." I find it funny he doesn't offer any words regarding their pleasant day spent together selling *olive* trees nor words of him returning as soon as possible to hang out with his-eager-to-share best friend.

Simeon picks up the slack in thoughtful words though. He seems to talk to Levi for days on end. Through the process I get bored and start to people-watch. I note three men without any luggage or carts coming through the gates. I could have sworn I saw one of them snatch a pomegranate from the street vendor and slip it under his cloak but I decide not to say anything about it. At last I hear Simeon stop for a breather and I turn to watch him embrace Levi one last time. Levi's goodbye seems intimate and images of him tending to Simeon that first day he arrived make my heart warm one last time.

Levi's goodbyes finally come to a close. To me, he simply nods his head, "Salome," to which I reply, "Levi." And with that, he is off, pulling at Nedra's reins.

I expect to feel some kind of sadness as I turn my back and start home again, but I believe the feeling is more related to relief. Thinking over the past week is kind of crazy now. It doesn't seem real that someone like Levi had been staying with us and that my family didn't even really know what all had happened on those tree-selling days.

I had planned on being more engaged in conversation with Josiah on the way home but as I review the last few days in my mind, I get lost in thought analyzing the actions Levi had taken toward me. I wonder why he touched me and how it could be he'd turned cold so quickly. I contemplate the effects of jealousy on men and what pride looks like when they wear it.

Wrapped up in my thoughts, I am completely surprised when I collide with the back of Josiah.

I'm quite familiar with the crowded streets of Jerusalem. I'm accustomed to bumping shoulders as you try to walk from one place to another. I'm used to carts occasionally rolling over your toes and chickens flapping in your face. The crowd we've caught ourselves in now seems no different. I can't make out much behind Josiah but it is noisy and I wonder if we have only stopped so Simeon can catch his breath. But as I begin to come back into reality, I realize the crowd we're in is not anything like ones I have been in before. It is noisy but the noise seems organized. Soon I can separate the shouts.

Ahead, there is a leader in the noise. He yells into the crowd about loyalty, honor and dignity. Two similar speeches are coming from two other men. These two voices are traveling however. Moving around and around the center voice, like minions.

Choirs start up in the crowd. To my left, one is singing in agreement with the three men. They shout things like, "We are loyal Jews! There are no troubles here so be on your way!"

Some behind me are singing praises. "Victory is with Barabbas!" "Damn the Pharisees! Damn the pacifists!"

To my right are pleads, more praises, more imploring, crying and shouting. "Damn the Sadducees!"

The man in the middle shouts, "They are all to be damned who are not zealous for the faith! The Romans will pay as will all who are faithful to them!"

The minions put forth a duet, "Barabbas will overthrow this government! One by one he and his followers will eliminate those who claim to be Jews yet act like second-rate believers."

"Will the real Jews not step forward and show their faith?" Barabbas spits. "Will we continue to live with imposters who disgrace *Yahweh* with their tolerant nature for the heathens that rule this holy city?!"

Some in the crowd cheer while I see others trying to escape through alleys and plead with shop owners to let them in. I start to sweat. I reach out for Simeon in front of me as a woman to my left shouts, "Who made *you* King of the Jews?!"

The crowd falls silent, but only for a second. The next moment is madness. Everyone to my left seems to have a sudden case of the jitters. Some ram into my side in an effort to escape the presence of the woman who spoke. Some rush into my other side trying to attack the woman. Others are rushing at me, and soon Simeon and Josiah are nearly falling over me.

I hear myself yelp as I crumble onto the Roman road, Simeon's cloak in my face. My yell is drowned out by the screams that surround me. One by one, a crescendo of screams emanate.

"That's the woman!" A man yells.

"This one deserves death too!" Another yells. "This is the one we saw conversing with the Samaritan!"

Josiah's voice is next. "No! Stop!"

I get anxious. I try to squirm out of the legs around me. I try to move my ankle out from under a woman who has crumpled to the ground, apparently unconscious. But screams are piercing my ears and throbs are echoing up my leg and my heart pounds in my ears. Then there is another blow to my head as someone tries to step over me but kicks me instead. Next, another body falls to my left at the feet of the already unconscious woman.

It is Simeon.

Once again I try to move. This time, someone steps on my hand, then another kick to the head.

I open my eyes again to see Josiah's back. He is hunched, kneeling over Simeon. I can't see Simeon anymore! *Move Josiah, move! What is going on!?*

"Stop! Stop!" I yell. "Stop! Let me up! Let me get to him! My brother!"

Desperation: when sanity holds no reason; when pride is no longer a virtue; when pleading is nature.

After multiple more kicks to the head, I accept defeat and curl into a fetal position until I know I can get up again.

I hear the soldiers arrive. I hear the thumping rhythm of their sandals and their leather straps smacking their thighs, clinking against their metal chests. They shout and yell and whip and push, pull, drag and beat people out of the streets.

I glance up in time to see groups of them restraining the three men, the one known as Barabbas and the two minions. The leader continues to yell about justice, loyalty and honor. One minion yells profanities at the soldiers that restrain him and he tries to spit in their faces. The other minion yells that he is sorry. He begs them to let him go and not to beat him.

I uncurl my body as a group of soldiers approach me. They stop to my left and scoop up the woman on my ankle. Blood drizzles from her nose and lands on my calf. I instinctively pull my leg in under my cloak and wipe at it.

More soldiers approach my left and stoop down at Simeon. This movement gives me strength enough to finally jump from my spot and land three feet over at Josiah's side.

"No, don't take him," Josiah holds his hand up to the closest soldier. "I'm here with him. I'll take care of him." I grab Simeon's shoulder and pull him toward me. As he rolls over I see his face is distorted into a permanent state of shock. His eyes are glazed over and wide as they can get. His mouth is the same way, slobbering and hanging.

He isn't moving. He isn't talking. He isn't blinking.

I can't hear Josiah. I can't hear the soldiers. I can't hear the clucking chickens or rolling carts, the distant screams or shuffling feet. The world is lost. I am in a parallel dimension, invisible to everyone. It is only me and Simeon. I try to hear a heartbeat. I try to hear a breath, a whisper, an anything.

I raise my hand to grab him at the waist, to shake him awake, to force him to pay attention to me, to make him stop resembling a zombie and to start looking like my brother again. But my hand lands in blood. A moist puddle of red is seeping out of his stomach, soaking into his tan cloak. I jerk my hand away and find myself zooming back to the world where Josiah is yelling, "He's not dead! Will you listen to me? I'm telling you I can help him!"

The nearest soldier slaps Josiah across the face. "You're being a fool! The boy is dead!"

Josiah rolls back off his heels onto his butt. A puff of dust rolls up over him and I see the wet streaks on his face leaving their path through the dust that is there. I recognize the look on his countenance—*defeat: the position you get in when you realize your fight is over and you are pointless, useless, worthless really, and there is no hope for impact, so just forget about it.*

The soldier beside him speaks up, "We'll leave him with you, kid. Make sure he's off the street."

And then they finally leave us alone.

Chapter Nine

It is like Josiah has turned into a robot.

It only takes seconds after everyone leaves us for him to blink once, pick up Simeon in one scoop, drape him over his shoulder, and begin walking home.

It takes me minutes to pick myself up off the street and follow him.

When I get home, Josiah is already walking back out the shop door, blood smeared up his front and down his arms. He blinks once when the door clanks behind him. He pauses for only a second to watch me take a step closer to the house. His chest is pumping up and down, yet his face stays as still as stone. When I'm only a step away from him he lunges his way down the street toward his house.

It only takes a second for me to grasp why Josiah came and went so quickly. He hadn't taken Simeon up to the loft. He is lying across a table in the shop. The pots that were once there are broken on the ground. Mom and Dad are draped over Simeon's body, wailing.

The rest of that day follows like the rest of that week. It vanishes in a blur that I don't really remember smelling or tasting or breathing. Simeon's body is eventually wrapped, spiced and placed in my dad's tomb. Of course, a tomb isn't ready for my 18 year-old brother, so he is placed beside my mother's tomb, where his old dad should be buried.

Josiah is there when we put him in. He helps my dad push the rock back in front of it and then they hold each other and cry.

Josiah is at the tomb the next day when I come to visit, and the next day after that, and the day after that one too. Each day, we sit on a boulder about 12 feet away from Simeon's tomb and stare at the rocks. Every day, he holds my hand and I hold his. It is mutual because we both are each trying to hold the other one together. When I get to the point to where I can't breathe from crying so hard, Josiah squeezes my hand, and when he starts to fall off the boulder from crying so hard, I clutch his in return. We don't talk to each other. My parents don't speak. No one has a voice. It looks like no one eats. I wonder if anyone will ever use their tongue again.

The 25th day at the tomb is the hardest. Josiah doesn't come. I try to sit there alone but I keep feeling like I am going to slide off the boulder and for some reason, it feels like Simeon isn't in there anymore.

On the 30th day, I decide to sit on the wall behind Beth and Eli's house. I look out over the city to where the road disappears over the bend toward Jericho. I see the exact spot where we left Levi. I follow the path up the hill, noting the same trouble-making chicken and young girls playing in the street.

Tears silently roll down my cheeks as I picture Levi leading Nedra with her cart of olive trees, my brother in the back. I can hardly see anything anymore with all the tears that have backed up due to the overflow of their traffic on my cheeks, but I still picture Simeon lifting his hand to wave at me. *Classic Simeon smile*, I think. Then my crying becomes noisy.

I cry so much my insides must look like a desert. There is no way any more water can still be in me. When I finally lift my face off my hands, it is dark outside, so I go home and curl up in bed, where miraculously more tears come.

Today, I face another surprise. Mom and Dad still have tongues to use. But still, when they talk, their voices crack as if they have just awaken, even though I think Mom and Dad don't sleep anymore either.

"Salome," Mother croaks. I look at her for only a second (it is all I can manage). She looks like a zombie now too. She has dark purple circles under her eyes and her face resembles ashes with wrinkles. Both my parents look like they've aged 50 years. My father's slouch is worse. He is curled over like a shepherd's cane, his eyes constantly studying his sandals. I think he glances at me each time I'm not looking at him, but

I don't want to hold eye contact with either of them until they appear human again.

I escape to Beth and Eli's backyard before they can say anything else. I sit on the wall. I rest there for a couple of hours trying to see anything new in the blue sky before Beth gets the better of my attention.

I can tell she is debating with herself if she should talk to me or not. She paces back and forth between her clothes lines but never hangs anything new up. She bites her lower lip then knocks her heels together before she makes her decision to approach me. I brace myself, ready to tell her to think twice if she thinks I shouldn't sit on her wall anymore.

Nonetheless, her voice, so shockingly gentle, surprises me. "Salome?"

I debate for a second if I should pretend I don't hear her or if I should jump and run, but finally I decide neither and turn to face her.

She looks me over and it seems to me she concludes I'm not dangerous, and she approaches me some more. She rests her arms on the top of the wall and leans into it. She looks at me for a few seconds and then follows my gaze out over the city. She is taller than what I have always thought. Up close I can see more silver in her hair than you would think. She has wrinkles around her eyes and freckles on her cheeks.

She stands there in the same position for a long time looking at the city with me. Then a feeling sweeps over me, sudden and unstoppable. It is this necessity to talk. It is like my tongue has found its fill of words at last and they have to be shared instantly.

"Simeon died. My brother, Simeon, did you know him?" I look at her and already the tears are flowing down my cheeks. I don't give her time to answer but she is nodding her head as I move on. "He was killed in the street, right down there. You see that man petting the brown horse down there?" I point. "It was just in front of him. My brother was the nicest person you'd have ever met. You probably did meet him. He talked to everyone. I'm sure he wouldn't have been able to live in front of you all his life and not talk to you. He talked to you, didn't he?" Once again, I don't leave time for an answer but Beth is still nodding her head.

"Thought so. I don't know how someone could kill the nicest person in the world, do you?" Beth shakes her head. "But someone did. I didn't see who. I didn't do anything. I was a good-for-nothing rag on the road that everyone kept stepping on." My voice catches and I choke on my spit.

"Some idiot just killed him! Stabbed him, I think. There was blood everywhere. He was covered in blood, Beth!" I look at her and I'm sure I seem like a crazy woman, but I can't stop now.

"Right in the gut! And you know what? You know what, Beth?" I pause a moment longer this time. Beth just stares at me.

"The guards just told us to clean him up off the street. Just to tidy things up like I'd made a mess. Like Simeon wasn't a real person. Like he was in the way. 'Yes, officer! Because it is my brother's fault he fell dead right here! How dare you, Simeon? Couldn't you find a better place to die?'" I talk to myself.

"And I don't even know them. I'm not acquainted with those guards. I'm not familiar with the men who were shouting. I don't know them from Adam and yet they took the most important person in the world from me." I have nothing more in me at this point so my head thuds into my palms and I shake with tears.

Beth's warm hand touches my spine and all my back muscles constrict, shaking with pain. I am stiff and sore. She rubs her hand up and down my spine. The warmth of her hand melts more of the tears out of me until finally I feel the hand is soaking them up for me.

I draw in one good, long breath and straighten up, taking in the bright sun through my swollen eyes. Beth stops rubbing my back and lets it rest in the center of my spine.

Sucking up some snot, I look at her. She looks tired too but not tired from a lack of sleep or a day of chores. She looks tired from hearing my speech, like my words are resting on her shoulders now. She too takes a deep breath and straightens up.

She removes her hand and starts to twiddle her thumbs. Then she speaks. "I'm sorry about Simeon, Salome. He truly was the most wonderful person in the world. I would agree."

A single tear rolls down my cheek and I nod my head in agreement.

"He said hello to me every day." She peers over the city as if she is looking for him, like I had been.

"Quite a few times, he stopped to help me hang some blankets," she half smiles. I picture Simeon doing just that and I half smile too.

"One time," she laughs a little, "it was in the winter season and he was helping me like he did, and he hung up a blanket, clothes pin here, clothes pin there," she acts out the scene in front her. "Well, I watched him because he just always had the greatest smile, and he was smiling when he hung up the last clothes pin and I saw what happened but I didn't say anything." She laughs a little more. "He hung his long sleeve along with the blanket and, when he turned to go, he found he was stuck." She laughs. "We just laughed so much. Simeon, he just couldn't stop laughing at himself and, once he got me going, he just kept doing silly things to keep me amused. By the time he left, I think everyone in town thought I'd gone mad from laughing so much."

We both smile at the thought of it all for a long time. When our smiles wear off, Beth meets my eyes.

"I think my son would have been like Simeon. Just like him."

I am sad inside on a whole new level but this kind of sadness feels healthier, like it is sadness for the right reason.

Beth puts her hand over top of mine. "I don't know why it is, things like this happen. Why it is God takes the best ones. Why he makes it so hard," she looks away. "But it is what it is. And I've been watching you, Salome." She looks back at me. "And I want to tell you something. There are two things that can happen. One," she holds up a wrinkled, swollen finger. "You can be like Simeon. You can make the best of this life. You can make people laugh every day and make them happy and glad they're living. You can smile," she points the finger at me. "You can get off this wall. Or two," she holds two fingers in the air, "you can end up like me." Shame crosses her face and she drops her fingers. "You can say nothing is ever going to be the same. That nothing will ever be alright again. You can stay angry at people and mad and hate them inside. But if you do, you'll end up alone and wishing you had ended this life before you had enough time to mess it up this badly. There are only two choices here, Salome. Be a Simeon, or a Beth." She shakes her head. "And Beth is telling you, Beth is not the right choice." Beth drops her eyes that are quickly filling with tears and she wipes her hands on her apron. She sniffles then rolls her shoulders back as she pulls up her head, recomposing herself. "Thank you," she pauses, "for talking with me."

Beth's eyes are the darkest brown I've ever seen, like her eyes have taken on the color of all the dark things she's seen in her life. Yet she holds her chin high now, restoring herself like a proper lady. She admits to being an unfit role model and yet she doesn't carry shame. It's like she doesn't have to because she knows she simply won't change so what is the point of shaming herself? I wish I had that kind of admission. That kind of confession just makes a person seem lighter, like Beth could walk on clouds because shame isn't weighing her down.

She walks a few steps before turning around again, "You remind me a lot of him, you know?"

I turn to look at her. "Your eyes—you have the same eyes." She nods as if she just figured it out for herself and then she turns, disappearing into her house.

I spin back around to the city, letting everything she said soak in. It takes me hours to go over it all but when I finally have, I look down at the wall I'm sitting on and I make my decision.

I get up.

Chapter Ten

Once I'm home, I make supper on my own. I insist that Mom sits down and lets me do it. She is surprised just like I knew she would be.

You know how they say people can't change in just one day? Well they can. I did. I am someone new. I feel new. I feel clean, better, like all the selfishness that has spoiled my insides for so long is suddenly sucked out of me. Perhaps Beth was the cure. I wonder if she had talked to me years ago if I would have changed then. I wish I could have traded all my self-pity and used sorrow for something worth feeling sad about. I wish I would have used it on Beth instead of myself.

I think about this while I cook and as I set the table and I probably would have thought about it all night but then I remember I need to talk to my parents.

I want to start from the very beginning. "I'm sorry."

They look up at me with their purple baggy eyes in amazement.

"I'm sorry I haven't been around here for you guys. I'm sorry I haven't been here at all. I know you two probably have a lot of questions and I," images start to run through my mind of that terrible day. My voice slows and I feel myself starting to disappear back to the scene. I stop myself. I remind myself I have to stay here. There is unfinished business to deal with. Confession is needed. "I haven't been around to answer any of your questions because I've been selfish." I force the words out. "I've always been selfish." Mom and Dad sit up straighter. "I've never cared about you guys like you care for me or how Simeon cared. I've never given anything to you. I've never tried to make you smile or laugh. I always relied on Simeon for everything. I knew he was enough to make everyone happy and so I just took rather than follow his example, I guess." I had thought a lot about how I was going to say all of this. Still, I had no idea it would feel this good.

"I want to start over, if I can. I want to be better. I want to live like Simeon. I'm here for you now." I reach my hands across the table, placing one on each of my parent's hands. Gentle tears roll down their cheeks.

Mom clears her throat and glances at my dad for a second, "We're very proud of you, Salome. We love who you are, who you've always been." She pulls her hand out from under mine and wipes her eyes.

Dad squeezes my other hand, "Are these realizations coming to you today because you happened to talk to Beth?"

My dad never ceases to amaze me at how much he knows. I don't bother to ask him how he does it. I just nod my head.

He removes his hand from mine too. "Beth is a nice woman. She's very wise. She should do more talking than what she does."

"She said Simeon talked to her a lot."

Mom and Dad nod their heads. I realize then that *I* may have been ready to talk about Simeon, but *they* may not.

"I'm sorry if you don't want to talk about him yet."

Mom bursts into tears. "No, Salome. Of course we do."

Dad cries too. "Yes, Salome. Talk about him as much as you want to."

I don't know how to feel. I don't know if it would be selfish of me to continue to talk about him and selfishness is a new thing I'm trying to avoid. So it's just quiet for a while as I try to think.

Dad speaks first. "We already know what happened by the way. Josiah explained."

My heart warms at the sound of his name. I miss him.

"Do you know who those men were?" I ask.

Mom straightens up. "I'm going to wash the dishes and clean up. I'm sorry, Salome. I just don't want to hear it again."

I nod my head in understanding.

Dad answers, "Yes, I do. While you've been out, a lot of people came by who helped answer a lot of my questions."

How I could have missed all these people is a surprise to me. I guess I was more gone than I had thought.

"This is what I know: there are some who believe this place, Israel, is the rightful place of the Jews." Dad rubs his temple. "How do I explain this? Israel *is* the rightful place for the Jews. You know this, don't you?"

I nod my head in agreement.

"The problem, Salome, is Israel doesn't really *feel* like it belongs to the Jews. It doesn't really."

"It's the Romans," I cut in.

Dad looks surprised that I know this. "Yes. But as Jews, we believe the Messiah is coming to overthrow the Roman government and restore Israel back to the Jews. And here, he'll make his kingdom."

I hear the cry of the woman at my left in the crowd the day Simeon died, *"Who made you King of the Jews?"*

"This was prophesied many years ago—many, many years ago. And people are getting impatient, Salome. They're ready for the Messiah to come in his glory. They're tired of being under the Roman thumb. So their solution is to kill the Romans and," Dad shakes his head, sadness flooding to the surface, "and they're killing any Roman sympathizers. Meaning, they're killing any unfaithful Jews."

A thousand voices fill my head again. I find myself standing in the crowd once more hearing various shouts all around me. *"They are all to be damned who are not zealous for the faith! The Romans will pay and all who are faithful to them!" "We are all devoted Jews here so be on your way!" "This one deserves death too. He was conversing with a Samaritan."*

"They thought Simeon was a Roman sympathizer?"

"As unbelievable as that is, yes. Josiah said a man yelled that Simeon deserved to die because he was talking to Levi, a Samaritan. Samaritans are different from us, Salome. You know this too. And most Jews hate them. To, to be talking to one of them, and to look like they were friends, much less, Simeon probably didn't look like a typical Jew. I guess they thought that made him unfaithful rather than kind or hospitable . . ." Dad trails off as his head lands in his hand and he shakes it with great grief.

"So, if any Jew is caught talking to non-Jews they're just going to kill them?" I ask angrily.

Dad lifts his head back up. "They expect complete devotion, Salome. If you're not a zealous Jew, you're not one at all in their book."

"Well, just because we talk to other people, because we're nice to them, doesn't mean we don't follow all the laws and worship *Yahweh* with reverence and everything else!" I start to yell. I take some deep breaths to calm myself.

Mother peers over her shoulder at me and Dad nods his head, "I know, Salome. I've raised you to understand that the most important part of being a Jew is that we love as God loves us."

Automatically, I recite a passage that comes to mind: *"You shall not take vengeance, nor bear any grudge against the sons of your people, but you shall love your neighbor as yourself; I am the Lord your God."*

Dad nods his head. "Some believe the way of the Messiah is to kill his enemies. They believe the Messiah will come as a great soldier. He'll overthrow the Romans with his army and this army is the faithful Jews. There's no need to keep around any half-hearted Jews, in their opinion, because half-hearted Jews won't have the loyalty it takes to kill the Romans."

"So they think they're doing the Messiah a favor?"

"Some of them think they *have* their Messiah."

I'm stunned, *"Who?* Who is their Messiah?"

"Barabbas."

A sharp pain penetrates my head like a brisk freezing wind. "You're lying." That is the only reasonable explanation I can come up with right now. That my soft-spoken, kind-hearted dad would have to be lying straight to his daughter's face. Even that seems more believable than people making *that man* a Messiah. "That man, who killed Simeon? They think that is the Messiah who will free Israel? How could anyone want to worship a murderer? I'd never stay a subject to a murderous king!"

"Barabbas fits their description of a Messiah." Dad quickly stops me. "He's here to overthrow the Romans so the Jews can have their land. He's taking action, as they want a king to do. He has many followers. He's creating an army." Dad hesitates before his next words, making sure I'm looking at him. "His army is called the *Sicarii*."

Translation: the dagger-men.

In my mind, I see Barabbas pull out a knife from his cloak and ram it through the soft spot of Simeon's stomach. I know my face is turning green, trying to hold in the puke that is sure to come up.

"They were making their rounds through Jerusalem, recruiting, when," Dad's voice shakes and Mother slouches over the water tub and begins shaking with tears, "when you stumbled into his propaganda," Dad finishes.

I have to leave the table. Supper is making its way back up my throat. "Excuse me."

Once outside, I vomit over the wall behind Beth and Eli's house. Then I stand there and let the cool night air heal my sweaty face. I stare over the city at the spot where Simeon had laid and, without even thinking, I begin to pray, "God, please help. Please bring peace to me." I shake my head trying to get the images of the terrible day to fall out of my mind. "Please, God. Let me become what my name says I am to be. Let me be someone I've never been before. Let me be peaceful."

I cry for a long while. I watch the moon go from my left side to over top Beth and Eli's house. When I find myself looking straight up at it, I start to wonder what else I could be looking at. I wonder if Simeon is just above the moon, looking at me. *I bet he has that classic Simeon smile on his face. Don't you Simeon?* At first I feel stupid for talking to him, but then I decide I don't care. It feels good. So, I tell him my plans in becoming more like him. I tell him I'm so thankful he left such a good example for me to follow and who to become.

"I'm sorry I wasn't more like that when you were here. I'm sorry I couldn't do anything before you died. I'm sorry I didn't spend more time with you when you were cooped up in the house. I'm glad you got the head bandage off before you died though. It was nice to see both of your eyes again. Did you ever notice that I have your eyes? That's what Beth says." I choke out my last words. "I miss you."

Chapter Eleven

After the breakthrough with my parents, another week passes—another week without Josiah. I hadn't realized how long it had been since I'd seen him. It's like he just disappeared. Worries, of course, start to flood my mind. So, I try to keep my mind too busy to think about him. I keep my body busy. I help Mom make every meal. I make another pitiful pot with Dad and help him clean up all the broken ones. By the end of the week, home is homier and my parents look healthier. They've resumed talking. Mom is back to sitting at her stool watching Dad sculpt and she's even left the house a couple of times to get some fresh air. To my amazement, I see her and Beth go for a walk and return with some flowers one day. Things seem to be getting better. The only downfall is I find I can't keep my body busy enough to keep my mind from missing Josiah.

As severely as I don't want to discuss it with Mom, I eventually can't hold it in anymore. "Where's Josiah, you think?"

Mom stops folding her blanket in midair. "Well, I imagine he's trying to live life like we are, Salome."

She starts folding her blanket again but her eyes are on me. "Yeah, I know. But annoying us by dropping by all the time used to be normal."

Mom smiles because she knows I'm trying to cover up my curiosity by sounding irritated with Josiah. "You could just walk to his house and find out."

I'm surprised Mom would suggest such a thing. That isn't a lady-like thing to do at all. It seems too intrusive, too persistent, and too forward. *Guys don't like that, do they?* Then again, it is *my* mom suggesting this. I believe the term Levi had used to describe my parents was "modern."

"No, I don't care really. I was just wondering if he said something to you about not wanting to come or something." I cling to some ounce of hope that he really had given an explanation for why he wasn't around anymore.

Mom starts folding another blanket. "He didn't say anything to me. Your father might know. *They're* the ones who have been talking."

When could Josiah have gotten by me without my notice and talked to Dad? Maybe she's referring to when he was here around the funeral time.

"You know, Josiah is quite a nice guy, Salome." Mother wears a mischievous smile. I escape before she gets anything valuable out of me.

I tell Dad I'm going for a walk as I try to shimmy out of the shop door but he stops me.

"And you're going alone?" he questions.

"I'm meeting up with someone," I lie. "We're going to walk for a while."

"Is it Beth from next door?"

"No."

Dad raises an eyebrow. "Who?"

I hesitate. *Who can I say that he'll believe I'm actually meeting up with? Bethany runs through my mind. Rebecca maybe? He'll never believe any of that.*

I have no choice but to confess. "Josiah."

Dad shifts in his chair a little. His eyes go back to the vase in front of him. He eventually nods his head. "Have fun."

Joy: a feeling that is a million times better when it comes unexpectedly.

I hadn't fully thought through what I was going to say when I ended up at his house but when I tried to, I'd nearly turn around, changing my mind. I don't want to turn around, so I decide not to think about it. I'd just go with the flow. Whatever happened, happened. At this point, people in this town knew not to expect normal from me. Besides, who would turn away a girl whose brother had just been murdered?

I can tell by the way all the townspeople are watching me from the corners of their eyes that they feel pity for me. *Look, there goes the only child now. Her brother was murdered right in front of her, the poor dear.* It is like I can hear their thoughts. But my stubborn side portrays itself. I refuse to fall into their pitied looks and walk through town like an injured little cub. I hold my chin high, set my jaw (which reminds me of Levi and I slightly loosen it again) and keep my eyes straight ahead.

When Josiah's house appears around the bend, my face blushes and instinctively I slow my pace. I study the shop, looking for any movement from Josiah's dad. His shop is built like my father's. It's knit into the surrounding shops, all blocked up like one solid wall. A single wooden door swings on old hinges by the lonesome wide window. The second story is their loft. Up there, Bethany, Josiah and his parents live.

As I get closer to the shop, I hear a ruckus. A couple of times I hear a tool fling across the shop and muttered, muffled words follow. This is probably a bad time to intrude by the sound of it, but people are standing in the street staring at me, so I go straight for the door.

The banging and muttering stop as soon I knock. It's awkwardly quiet for many seconds before I hear his voice, "Yes. It's open. Come on in!"

I swallow my fear in one gulp and cross the threshold. It's messy and dusty, like my dad's shop. The difference is the materials. Where my dad has sculpting blades, Josiah's dad has needles with various threads hanging from the loops. Sheets of leather are strung over each of the tables. Some of them are soaking, some being dyed, some are being stretched and some of them are in the process of being hemmed.

He lays down a block of wood he's been using to stretch his latest piece of leather. He looks surprised. "Salome. What are you . . . how can I help you?"

He makes his way around the tables and stands only a few feet from me. I'm certain I've been in the cart numerous times when my parents would agree to Simeon and Josiah's sleepovers, but still I realized I had never spoken to him before.

He is dirty. His clothes have patches of leather dye on them and one of his shirt sleeves is stitched at the shoulder with his leather material. But his face is handsome. He is his own kind of character. He makes me feel like I'm not in Jerusalem anymore. He has bright blue eyes, an almost unheard of trait, and his brown hair is long, drawn back in a ponytail. I decide right away I like him.

"Hi, I'm sorry I disturbed you."

He looks around his messy shop and smiles. "No, not at all." He leans back against one of his tables and half sits on it. "What are you up to today?" He reaches for an apple on the table and tosses it back and forth between his hands. "My name is Ramen, by the way."

My face blushes. He must have caught on that I didn't know his name. *How embarrassing!*

"I realize we know *of* each other, but I don't think we've ever been properly introduced." He carries on without a care in the world. "I feel like I know you pretty well though if I do say so myself. Your dad always talks up a storm with me when he visits. Tells me all about you kids. And of course I know Simeon. I've spent enough time with him to think of him as my own son." He laughs but then stops tossing the apple.

I know he's probably rethinking his present tense verbs so I decide to jump in before the crying and apologizing come. "I'm actually here to see Josiah."

He looks up in surprise so I quickly add, "If that is okay."

As Ramen bites into his apple, juice trickles down his chin. "Yes, yes, of course, only I don't think he's here." My heart sinks. "I think he's at his uncle's herding sheep."

I nod my head and begin to accept my fate. "Come on, I'll show you." Ramen jumps from the table and starts walking to the back of his shop. I stand dumbfounded for a second. Ramen waves his hand at me when he reaches the back door. My feet kick into gear and I follow him out.

The view from their back yard is stunning. Just over the Roman wall a long pasture of green spreads down the valley to the left and up a hill to the right. Straight ahead it was like you can see for miles. Rolling hills eventually spread out to a flat line in the distance, the sun only an inch above it.

"If you follow this path down the valley it will take you around a bend by that tree down there, you see it?" He points and I nod. "It's only a half a mile or so after that tree you should see Josiah and his herd. He's making his way to this valley here. The sheep are going to graze here for a couple of weeks and then he'll move them on," he points up the hill to the right. "It'll be nice for him to have them so close. Night duty will be a lot more comfortable when he can watch them from the loft in his bed." His thumb goes over his head back to the house. Then he pats me on the shoulder. "If you don't want to walk there alone I can go get Bethany."

Bethany. I had forgotten about her. Images of her standing behind Josiah as she gawked at Simeon come back to me. I hear her screeching laugh and say, "No thank you. It doesn't look that far. I think I'll be okay."

"Alright, I'll tell MaryAnn to keep an eye on you from the loft." He pats my shoulder again. "Good to finally meet you, Salome. See you later." I smile at him until he disappears back through the door.

The walk through the valley is beautiful but I also feel awkward knowing Josiah's mom is watching me, and probably Bethany too.

Bethany. I think to myself. *You know you two are probably going to have to be friends if you marry her brother. Wait! Marriage? Did you seriously just use that word, Salome?* My mind scolds me. *Who are you these days? I mean, one day you can't stand Josiah, the next day you're hanging out with a Samaritan supermodel, and now you think you want to marry Josiah?* I laugh at my inward battle and take the bend around the tree.

Another wide clearing is there. It is vibrantly green and so beautiful I have to stop and stare. I wonder how it is I can live so close to this kind of beauty but remain trapped in the city like a rat.

Ahead I see white puffs hovering over the grass. To the left of the sheep is Josiah's silhouette. He stands with a long cane, curved at the top in case any sheep get tangled in hard to reach thorny places. He walks to a sheep, strokes it for a while then walks to a tree and sits down, his back resting against it. I get off the path and head straight to him.

He spots me about twenty yards away and quickly gets to his feet. "Salome?"

I wave. I don't know how it's possible but my heart is in my throat.

"What are you doing out here?" He props his cane against the tree and heads toward me.

We stop when we're feet apart. He's smiling at me, a Simeon-like kind of smile. "Your dad showed me the way."

We're quiet for a minute just glancing at each other. Josiah finally drops his gaze and looks over the field. "It's beautiful, huh?"

I look around too. One sheep in particular is gawking at me, grass hanging from its mouth. "Yes, it is."

"See why I like it so much? Shepherding I mean. It's quiet and you've got a great view."

I laugh because my great view is currently of a sheep staring me down, slobber starting to fall from its lip. "Yeah, you can't get tired of looking at sheep all day. Check out that one! It's just staring at me!"

Josiah follows my finger and bursts into laughter too. "She must be stunned by your beauty or something, huh?"

I feel my face blush and I turn so he can't see it full on. Then he pushes my shoulder. "Or maybe she's shocked that your feet are as dirty as hers."

I feel my heart relax. "Or maybe she's just surprised to see a girl here on her own free will."

"That reminds me," Josiah inquired, "why are you here again?"

"I haven't seen you in so long I was checking what my chances were that you moved to another country or fell into a thistle bush saving a sheep."

"Darn the luck, huh?"

"Darn it all."

We smile. "Well, while you're here you want to meet my family?"

At first I think he means Ramen, MaryAnn and Bethany but then he starts walking toward the sheep. Once again I feel relief.

His herd only has 16, which he explains is a small handful in retrospect. But his uncle hadn't wanted to start him off with too much given this being his first time shepherding and all. He had named each one. I honestly couldn't tell a difference in them but I thought it was cute, nonetheless.

"And that's Shoshanna the sheep, #16. I like to say that five times fast."

I give it a shot and let's just say it is terrible. Josiah and I just end up laughing again.

Then he shakes his head at me. "I didn't expect this."

I'm taken off guard. "What?"

"For you to be happy."

I nod my head because I know that is a reasonable expectation. Then I shrug my shoulders. "Beth from next door gave me a good talking to. I guess it opened my eyes to things." I thought of my eyes then. I hoped Josiah could see that I had the same eyes as Simeon. "But to be fair, I didn't expect this from you either."

"Expect what?" he asks.

"For you to not come around anymore."

He kicks at a clump of grass, "Didn't think you'd notice."

I don't know why it is but I am suddenly angry he is being so naive. "Don't be stupid, Josiah." I want to say more but I don't know how.

"I thought you may not want to see me."

"Why would you think that?" I probe.

He looks out over the valley. "Because I thought it would make you think of Simeon and," he kicks at the grass again, "I thought you wouldn't want to think about that."

Once again, it was a fair assumption. But . . . "But I saw you every day for the next three weeks or something. Remember that? Remember holding my hand on the boulder? You think I'd just want to never see you again after that?"

He looks into my eyes. "I'm sorry."

"Why did you do that? Why'd you just stop coming?"

"I couldn't do it anymore, Salome. I couldn't sit on the boulder and stare at my best friend's grave anymore. And I couldn't sit there and hold my best friend's sister's hand and not know what he'd feel if he saw me doing that."

Josiah turns a bright shade of pink in the center of his cheeks. I'm overwhelmed. I hadn't realized all of this would bother him.

I don't know what to do. We stand there in silence for a minute, both of us looking out over the valley.

"I tried to ask him one day."

His words catch me off guard. I don't know what he is talking about. I look at him puzzled.

"One day in the loft when Levi was here. It was the day we sold the trees." I still don't understand what he is talking about. Josiah reads my confused expression.

"It bothered me the way he touched you."

Memories of that day come flooding back to me.

"When I turned around and saw him rubbing on your arm like he was," his voice shakes, "like he owned you or something."

I feel shameful again. I can't speak and I can't look at Josiah anymore. I turn and stare at Shoshanna the sheep, # 16.

"I mean, didn't it bother you?" Josiah steps in front of me so I have to look at him.

I shrug my shoulders, "Yes, I guess. But what was I supposed to do about it? And how was I supposed to know it would bother you?"

"That's why it bothered me, because you couldn't do anything about it. And because you didn't know it *did* bother me."

The heat of my anger turns to affection. "Why did it bother you?" I think I know the answer, but I long to hear it with all my heart.

Josiah turns on his toe again, "Don't be stupid, Salome."

Every ounce of me smiles inside. Then I remember he'd gotten off track from his story. "So you tried to ask Simeon that day?"

"Oh yeah," Josiah turns back to face me. "I was venting about what I saw with Levi being all handsy and I guess Simeon caught on to my jealousy. He just started laughing at me even though I was so angry I could've blown my top off. You know how Simeon was. He just smiled and told me if I liked you I should make it known so other foreign guys wouldn't get any ideas about you. So I was going to ask him if it would bother him but then your mom came up."

First I note his proper use of the past-tense and then I let the second part sink in: Josiah just said out loud that he likes me. I'm sure he could see my heart pounding out of my cloak. But I have confidence now. "So, why don't you?"

Josiah looks like the puzzled sheep now.

"Why haven't you ever said anything?" I repeat.

I don't think either of us was prepared for this conversation. Josiah continues to look stumped.

"I guess I've tried to show you in my own way."

I laugh. "Like by comparing me to poop?"

Josiah laughs out of embarrassment, "No. I think it is fun that we can pick on each other is all. I guess it's my way of flirting with you."

A mixture of joy and pity come to me. "I honestly was never flirting with you, Josiah. I thought you legitimately were a turd."

Josiah shakes his head. "Yeah, that's why I never told you. I thought you'd think I was an idiot. I mean, someone like you liking someone like me?" He half laughs but I can tell he's sad at his words. I'm sad at them too.

"Are you kidding me? 'Someone like me?' What does that even mean? 'Someone like me.' I've always been difficult and not nice and definitely not like-able."

Josiah reaches for my hand then and for the first time I actually realize I'm holding it, not as a favor, not for healing, but because I want to.

He curls his fingers through mine. "Don't be stupid."

Chapter Twelve

A week has passed without a single thing going wrong. It seems everyone likes the new me much more. I'm able to make Mom and Dad laugh. I find I actually enjoy preparing meals and hanging out with Dad in the shop. I still think I'm terrible at pottery but I produce two more pots and Dad puts them in the shop window on display. I tell him it will be a miracle if they sell and he says "I've seen crazier miracles happen." I think he is talking about me in his secret-talking-about-more-than-what-you-think way. He may even be talking about the impossible miracle of Josiah and me. It is completely obvious by now that I have taken a liking to him. We've seen each other almost every day this week. When I think we have nothing more to talk about, Josiah has another great conversation-starter.

"Salome, tell me about how you came to believe Jesus is the Messiah."

We sit with our backs leaning up against the rock wall behind his house as we overlook the valley and the spots of white sheep.

"It's kind of a long story."

Josiah simply repositions his legs, stretching them out before him. When he smiles, I know it is time for my story to begin.

I tell him everything I can remember about the wedding and playing tag with Simeon. I explain to him in detail the person of Jesus, or who I imagined he looked like. And I reveal to him about Jude and Matthew, our murdered brothers, and the cart ride home. I even tell him about Simeon's talk with me that night about the Exodus and how it all tied together. Josiah never interrupted. He is a good listener. If I've learned anything about him the past couple weeks, it is this. He enjoys listening to people, or at least to me. Just like Simeon. He makes you feel like you can open up to him all your darkest secrets and never fear that he will scold you. He makes you feel like you are the only person around. I start to see that Josiah was probably born this way just like Simeon was and it was for this reason that they were best friends. Not that Josiah had learned it all from Simeon, as I had assumed before.

That day, I don't get to ask Josiah about his belief in Jesus of Nazareth because my own story brings so many of his own questions.

The next day I start the conversation saying, "Today is your turn. I want to know about how *you* believe in Jesus, and I'm going to listen."

This day we were moving the sheep further up the hill behind his house. We're almost too far away for my parents to let me continue joining him. So we take our time walking up the hill and, when we reach the top, we sit leaning against a tree and Josiah tells me his story. From his opening statement, I know it is going to be a story worth listening to.

"I was in Galilee too when I first met Jesus," he begins. "But that isn't where I first started to believe in him." I wrinkle my eyebrows.

"I first believed Jesus was the Messiah the day after you did." I want so badly to interrupt with a thousand questions.

"Your brother told me about the wedding in Galilee the day after you got home. He told me about tag and hiding under the table and how the voice of Jesus was the sweetest thing he'd ever tasted. He told me about you and the look on your face." I blush, wondering if Josiah liked me that many years ago.

"The way he described Jesus, Salome, I just knew he was something special. And the way Simeon changed. I mean, Simeon was always kind and gentle and happy, but after that day, he got serious too. We always used to joke and run around town picking at people and talking about nonsense all the time. And, don't get me wrong, we continued to do a lot of that, but after that day, he always wanted to study and talk more. We'd run through town to stir up old man Phil's chickens and then he'd want to stop by the synagogue. We'd catch pieces of the scroll reading and then we'd go find a place to talk about it for an hour. It was fun." Josiah seems to get lost in thought. He gazes over the valley for a moment. Then he breathes in deeply and continues.

"Simeon was for real about Jesus and I looked up to him. I believed everything he told me." He laughs. "I'd have believed him if he said a toad was a king!" I smile, knowing I am the same way.

"No, I never doubted Jesus was the Messiah from the moment Simeon told me he believed he was. Your brother had a way of explaining things," Josiah says as he looks deeply into my eyes. "He could explain something to you, not seeming to try to make you believe anything, and yet in the end, that's exactly what you did." I nod my head in agreement.

"I'm eternally grateful to your brother."

We are quiet for a while, just studying each other. I don't know what he is thinking about, but I look at him to imagine the change my brother must have made in him. I try to picture him as a non-believer. I wonder if it would physically change his appearance. I think it would. I think he'd look less bright, more dim and unhappy. I miss Simeon a great deal then.

Josiah eventually nods his head, with his goofy smile appearing again. Then he continues, "So I didn't need any further evidence but I got it. My dad's father passed away last year. They weren't close or anything but my dad still went up to give his mom some money and things to just kind of help her out I think. All of us decided to go with him. We stayed one night with his mother in the house he grew up in and the next morning he was ready to go. We were just strolling along. Dad and I were leading the donkey through the city. Bethany and Mom were in the cart. We were almost out of the town gate when this large crowd started approaching. I was trying to figure out who it was when Dad nearly tore off my shawl trying to get me to stop. I hadn't realized it but I almost walked straight into a funeral procession." His story just kept getting better and better.

"That's when I realized everyone around us was dead quiet, you know, showing their condolences. We stopped and watched them carry out the coffin. By the time they got through the gate, a large crowd was there. I saw this man approaching one of the women there. He kind of had to stop and wave off all of these guys who were following him. It was like they were his body guards. But this one lady there," Josiah shakes his head as if it is painful to picture it, "she was just wailing with everything in her. She was crying so hard she was practically screaming." Josiah swallowed hard.

"Then the man walked up to her. I couldn't tell what he said but as soon as he put his hand on her shoulder the lady seemed to wake up. She stopped crying and they just looked at each other for a while. By then, everybody was completely quiet. The guys put down the coffin and we all just watched. The man lifted up his hand and started wiping the tears off the lady's face. Then he just looked at her. I realized then that this guy had eyes like fire and I knew, I just *knew*, it was Jesus."

Goosebumps appear all over my flesh.

"Then he said to her, 'Don't cry.'"

Josiah turns to look at me. He has a mystical look in his eyes I'd never seen before. The tip of his nose is turning red. It looks like he is going to cry.

"Simeon was right. His words were so gentle, so quiet it was like the birds had stopped to listen to him." He turns to gaze out over the valley again. "He walked up to the coffin and told the guy to get up." He looks at me with amazement now. "He just said, 'Get up, young man!' And I'm not kidding, Salome, the dead guy got up!" My heart began to accelerate.

Josiah jumps up, "The guy was in his burial cloth and, when he stood up, the rag on his face just fell down." Josiah shakes his hands in the air, "But he didn't look like a dead nasty old body. He looked like a regular kid. He couldn't have been much older than me, Salome, and he looked just fine."

My brain starts to feel overloaded with information. I try to absorb Josiah's happy energy but a poisonous feeling soaks into my toes and makes its way up to my guts.

"Then Jesus grabbed the guy's hand and helped him out of the coffin." Josiah continues to talk but his voice is getting more distant. The toxin is filling in my ears. I take my eyes off him and stare at the ground.

"He took him over to the lady who was crying and it turns out he was her son! The whole crowd went wild. Everyone started chanting different things." Josiah bounced back and forth between characters, acting out the scene, "'Hail Jesus, King of the Jews!'" He whistled and cupped his hands to make the sound of a roaring crowd. I began to feel annoyed with his excitement and forgetfulness.

"Josiah stop," I finally blurt out.

He lets his hands fall from around his mouth. "What? What's wrong?" Noticing my poisoned face for the first time, he sits beside me.

"Don't you see what this means?" I know I am looking at him too critically but it seems like my face can't help itself. "If Jesus can raise people from the dead, why doesn't he raise Simeon?"

Josiah takes in my words like he'd never thought such a thing before. He starts shaking his head back and forth. "I hadn't realized you were thinking about that. I, I'm sorry. I didn't connect that with Simeon."

He continues to stammer out sentence fragments but I stop listening to him. Anger brews inside me and my head starts to shake. "Why wouldn't you think about that? That would have been the first thing I thought of."

Josiah looks truly hurt. "I didn't think of it because I've never thought about wanting Simeon back from the dead."

I can't believe it. *He doesn't want his best friend back anymore?! Was he this completely selfish that as long as he got his best friend's sister he didn't care if Simeon ever lived again?*

"How could you say that?" is all I can manage.

Josiah starts to sweat. "Salome, do you realize how selfish it would be of me to *want* him back here?"

I start to get up. I just had to escape. I need to walk around to let the wind dry up the sweat that has formed on my face as well.

Josiah pulls me back down by the arm, "Don't go. Listen to me."

I will myself to stay but I have to shut my eyes as tightly together as possible.

"I wouldn't be much of a friend if I wanted Simeon to come back here to this earth where he can feel the pain of his attack again all over his body, now would I? I don't want him back here when he is no doubt completely happy where he is. He's not just lying in some tomb, Salome."

My eyes open and Josiah is holding both of my shoulders in his hands, his arms like bars, holding me to face him. "He's not rotting away in there. I don't care what other people say about it. I just know in my heart that Simeon is with God. I don't believe his soul is stuck behind that rock." He lets his arms fall away from my shoulders but his eyes stay on mine, hoping they'd be enough to keep me there.

I try to let it all soak in, all these ridiculous beliefs Josiah just threw up on me. As a Jew, I don't know much about what happens after death. I don't know if there is a heaven right away or not. I just know there is a judgment. A final judgment will come by the Messiah himself and then everyone will be resurrected, physically, into heaven with their Messiah. This heaven will be new and perfect, but did it already exist for those who are dead? I had never imagined that before.

I try to think why it is I can talk to Simeon every night under the moon. Why I feel like he is there. And I can't imagine Simeon in a great deal of pain as he listens to me. I picture him as he was before the attack on the road to Jericho. I see him perfect, with his Simeon smile and wavy brown hair. I see him in a clean cloak and flowing shawl.

Josiah interrupts my thoughts. "Do you not feel like in some way Simeon is here with us now? Like he has been since he left?"

My eyes search Josiah's as fervently as his search mine. It is like we are trying to find truth in each other.

I've never cared what others thought before so why start now? If I want to believe Simeon was already with God I could if I wanted. It makes me feel better to picture him up above the moon rather than in a dark clammy tomb. I don't even care if I'm wrong. So I nod my head.

Josiah's face relaxes tremendously. He sighs and leans back against the tree. "I don't know if I'd even ask Jesus to bring him back to life, Salome. I'd just feel too selfish. I mean, I don't know if that's what Simeon would even want."

The venom slides back out through my toes. I start to feel peace again. I begin to feel courtesy toward Josiah, then I feel badly I had gotten mad at him.

"I'm sorry."

Josiah turned to me, "For what?"

"For getting mad so quickly. I just had never thought about it that way before. I guess I'm naturally more selfish."

Josiah starts shaking his head, "No, Salome. You're not selfish. I wish you could see the way you've changed like I have. I mean, the difference in who you are from a couple weeks ago to now is so incredible. You have every right to be selfish and instead you've changed into the most beautiful spirit." Josiah cuts himself off like he is saying more than he has intended.

While he blushes, I let his words register with me. They penetrate me and wait for me to choose if I want to believe them or kick them out. I look at the words for a moment and I don't personally believe they are true, yet I decide I want them to stay. I want the change to be true, but I have to admit something.

"I don't think I'm that selfless still, Josiah. I still think if I had the chance, I might want Simeon back whether or not he wanted to leave God and heaven and all that." I am still confused by my own words regarding the afterlife but I let it come out. I know Josiah is the safest place to explore this new belief.

Josiah just nods his head. "Now that you've brought it to mind, I think I'd debate it too if I see Jesus again."

I feel relieved, knowing my selfishness must have been an okay amount to have if Josiah had the same thought I did. Instantly I felt better, like all the toxin was miles away.

"Now if it was you on the other hand," I start to joke, "I think I'd let God keep you."

Josiah laughs. "Well thanks, Salome. Same to you."

The rest of that day ran a lot smoother. There was no more discussion of death and the afterlife. We kept the conversation light and we found ways to make each other laugh. I threw dirt clods at him when he wasn't looking and he jumped out from around some trees to scare me. Then we'd chase each other around and use the sheep as blockades. And like each night before, I was sad to hear "Shalom."

Chapter Thirteen

N ow I sit with Dad on the front step of our shop door. Josiah is well beyond the hill behind his house now so I'm not able to venture with him on his shepherding duties anymore. Not until the herd is brought back around to graze there again or somewhere nearby. So Dad and I have started another pot in the shop. We've just taken a lunch break and have decided to let it settle while we sit in the sunshine.

Sitting here isn't the greatest idea. As people scurry by, dust stirs up and we are at just the right height for it all to fly in our faces. But both us are feeling too lazy to move once we sit down. We just wave our hands in front of our faces until the swirl of it dies down. We say hello to Beth and Eli. We nearly have our toes run over by a cart. Then while we're having a contest throwing pebbles at a dried worm in the middle of the street, Roberta appears. Jerusalem is a big town. With this in mind, it probably isn't quite fair to call Roberta "the town gossip," but I won't deny that it could actually be accurate.

"Did you hear what happened in Bethany?!" Roberta croaks. She runs up the street in a stupor, stirring dust into our faces. She is going so fast she holds up the corner of her cloak in one hand, almost clear to her knee, showing off her varicose veins.

Roberta has a nose too large for her face. It's shaped like a hill, giving her the appearance of a parrot. This bird-like quality only makes her more animated (given the job of a parrot is to repeat whatever it hears). It is for this reason Roberta is always half-heard by most people in Jerusalem. Usually what she has to say has already been said at some point. The only people who listen are those who haven't heard the news beforehand.

She runs right past Beth to Sarah who lives next door. There are some people Roberta knows not to gossip with. Beth and my mother are some of those ladies. They show no interest in the business of the town. I find myself blessed to have inherited the same trait as my mother.

Sarah is pouring her water bowl out in the alley of the street. "What is it, Roberta?" she asks.

Roberta drops her cloak and huffs and puffs for some breaths before she begins. "Lazarus, of Bethany, the brother of Mary and Martha. . . " She puts her hands on her hips and sighs, frustrated for not being able to tell her story more quickly because she is so out of breath. "He's been raised from the dead!"

Sarah drops her water pot and it shatters on the ground. My heart stops and my head turns to Roberta to make sure I have heard her correctly. This time I *am* going to listen to her.

"No! What do you mean 'Raised from the dead'? He's been dead for five days now." Sarah shakes her white head of hair.

"Yes! Yes, it's true." Roberta waves her hands in the air like a parrot flapping in a cage. "I just heard it from Phil's wife, Naomi."

Sarah shakes her head. "That isn't possible . . ."

Roberta cuts her off. "It is too! Jesus of Nazareth, the one the crowds have been following around, he was there. He was the one who did it. There are eye witnesses and everything."

I am locked in on their conversation now. I have to know every detail. Inside, I beg for Roberta to carry on.

"Well of course there are eye witnesses. How else would you know about it?" Sarah seems less interested in the fact that a man has just come back to life and more interested in still being smarter than her gossiping friend.

Roberta bobs her head with attitude. "Well, I'm surprised you haven't heard about it yet, Sarah."

Sarah and Roberta start talking at the same time then about who knows more about the city than the other. They rant about who has lived there longest and how long their family line goes back through

Jerusalem. I can't help myself any longer. I get up from the step and make my way to them.

"Excuse me. What was it you were saying about Jesus of Nazareth?"

Both women stop talking immediately and gaze at me, calculating me as the teenager they know I am. Both look skeptical yet they can't help themselves but share their "knowledge."

"Lazarus of Bethany was brought back to life yesterday." Roberta informs me slower than she had Sarah as if I might not understand every word.

"And you said he'd been dead for four days?"

Roberta puts her hand on her hip. "Yes. Hadn't you heard when he died?"

I try not to let anger fill me. "How do you know this? Who did Naomi hear it from?"

Roberta looks shocked that I would question her sources but Sarah puts a hand on her hip and looks at Roberta questioningly too.

"Naomi didn't hear it from anyone, child." Roberta shakes her head. "She was there herself."

Sarah and I gasp at the same time.

"You don't say!" Sarah jumps in. "What was she doing in Bethany?"

Roberta looks proud to know more information than Sarah again. "Well don't you know Phil trades some of his chickens with his cousins there in Bethany? They go every six weeks or so."

Sarah perches her lips. I jump in before more arguing about who knows who better can resume. "Can you tell me everything Naomi saw?"

Both look surprised again. "Naomi was only a half a mile or so away from the tomb Lazarus was buried in. That's where Phil's cousin lives," she says to Sarah then turns back to me. "She said they were about to leave to come back home when they saw this huge crowd heading toward the tomb, just a hillside over. So they decided to see what it was all about, you know?" She nods at me and Sarah. "When she got there, Jesus of Nazareth was talking to Martha, the eldest of Lazarus' sisters." She points out to Sarah again. Sarah looks annoyed.

Roberta changes her tone to a more feminine voice: "Jesus, if you had been here my brother wouldn't have died," Roberta acts out the scene before us. Faking some sobs, she continues to mimic Martha.

"But I know if you ask God he'll give you anything." Roberta jumps out of character. "That's what Naomi heard Martha say to Jesus." Roberta switches character voices. Now in a deep voice she whispers, "Your brother will rise again, Martha."

"Oh, stop all this acting, Roberta, and just tell us what Naomi said," Sarah complains.

Roberta rolls her eyes and puts her hand back on her hip. "Then Naomi said Martha started telling Jesus she knew Lazarus would rise again on Judgment Day with the rest of us but that wasn't exactly what she was talking about. So, Jesus told her *he* was the resurrection and *the life.*" Roberta bobs her head more severely this time.

At this point, Dad has come to my side to listen in as well. Roberta carries on as if she doesn't see him. "Then he told the whole crowd that whoever believes in him will never die because *he* is the Son of God."

Sarah's mouth drops open. "He did not."

"Oh, yes he did." Roberta nods her head so the whole town can tell she's saying yes. Dad shifts his weight behind me.

"Then Mary, the younger of the two sisters, came over to him and said, 'If you had been here, my brother wouldn't have died.'"

Sarah nods her head, "That's what I would have said too."

"Well, you won't believe this," Roberta talks squarely to Sarah now. "Jesus just started crying."

My heart sinks to the pit of my stomach.

"No," Sarah gawks again.

"Yes," Roberta looks at all three of us now. "Then he went over to the tomb and told them to take away the stone. And honey, you should have seen Naomi's face when she was telling me this. She got white as a ghost. Can you imagine what the smell would have been like?"

Anger flares up in me. How is it these two women can talk about how a dead man's body smells out of all this? How stupid could you be to pick to focus on that bit of the conversation out of all that is about to happen? I try to swallow.

"Then Jesus told the crowd what he was about to do was all for the glory of God, *his Father.* I personally, don't know how anyone could have stayed around after opening up the tomb like that. I would have fainted from the odor."

Roberta wrinkles her nose at me like I will agree with her. I want to punch her hill-of-a-nose. Thankfully she continues before I lose my temper.

"Then he turned to the grave and said, 'Lazarus! Come out here!' It took Naomi an hour to tell me just that, she was shaking so much."

Roberta and Sarah continue to talk about Naomi's health while I try to keep my balance. I feel light headed. I feel like the world is slightly tilting and I am going to tip over. I feel sick. The poison enters through my brain this time and is making me delusional.

"He told the guys there to take off his grave clothes just like that. And what do you know? The whole crowd saw Lazarus walking and talking like he'd never been dead a day in his life."

I have to walk away from them. I have to find a place to sit. I have to find a place to be alone. Dad touches my arm but before I can process anything, my body jerks away from him. I don't even know what it is that is bothering me so much until I'm alone in the loft. I ask Mom to leave and I shrink under my sheets on my cot. I think I'm going to hyperventilate for a few minutes so I close my eyes and try to focus on breathing in and out. Eventually, my heart slows so much I can't feel it in my chest. I liked that feeling. I suddenly don't want a heart. I want nothing in my system. I want nothing but emptiness so I won't have to feel anymore. I don't want to care. I don't want to know what to care about. I don't want anything but Simeon now. And with this realization of the one thing I want, I realize another: I don't want God and I especially don't want the man who claims to be his Son.

I don't know how it is possible but I manage to fall asleep shortly after curling under my blankets. When I wake up, I can hear my parents talking beneath me in the shop. Their voices carry up through the wooden floor.

"I don't know, Joan. I think it could have been the conversation Sarah and Roberta were having that upset her," Dad says.

"What, with the talk about Lazarus?" *How had she heard what they were talking about?*

"Yes. She was very interested in it. She kept asking Roberta about it. She said she wanted every detail Naomi gave her. Then she just stormed off."

Mother was silent for a minute. Now I'm fully awake.

"Do you think she's upset about Lazarus coming back to life when Simeon is . . ." her voice trails off and I imagine Dad holding her as she quietly cries.

Dad's voice was barely audible. "That's the only thing I can think of."

"Well, what are we going to do, Matthew? She's been up there for almost three hours now. We can't just avoid her or pretend this didn't happen."

Dad sighs. "I know, my love. How about we go talk to her together?"

I perk up at this and start to squirm in my blankets. I wonder if I should pretend to be asleep again. Would they leave me alone then and decide to never talk about this? I don't even know what to say yet.

But before I can do anything, pretend to sleep or come up with a fake reason for my hiding, my parents are entering the loft.

I flip the sheet off me and turn to face them. For a brief second I wonder why I have to do this. Why do I have to return to my old self? Why do I have to let this bother me? Why can't I pretend to be happy and carry on with making my parents smile like I have been for the past few weeks? Weren't those weeks the greatest ones I've had in a long time? *Yes, they were,* my mind answers my heart. *And they were foolish and blind is what they were.* My heart cowers from my mind. *I actually thought God wasn't to blame. I thought there was such a thing as "transcendent peace." Now, my eyes are open, you stupid heart, and I can see that God is a scam. He sends some guy to raise people from the dead with his secret magic stuff and ignores the rest of the world. Some God!*

Mom and Dad sit on the cot, one on each side of me. Both of them grab a hand. I brace myself and my brain tells my body to be strong, to be stiff. He orders my skin to put up every protective barrier possible against feeling and emotion. *Damn the eyes! We won't have any tears escaping today!* He orders. *And ears, get ready to shut down on my command.* Then he tells my heart to shut up. He locks it behind the bars of my rib cage in a place that will be hard to find later and tells me to swallow the key.

"Honey, do you want to tell us what's wrong?" Mom puts on her gentle pleading voice (the voice she uses when we're sick). She used it the whole time she talked to Simeon after he arrived all bandaged up from his attack.

"No."

Mom and Dad exchange troubled looks. I know better than to expect it to be this easy though.

"Well, we want some kind of explanation for why you kicked your mother out of the loft, Salome." Dad tries to use his stern voice, but he really doesn't have one.

I roll my eyes. "I wanted to be alone."

"Why?" they both ask at the same time.

"Because I just did, okay? I'm not happy." I pull my hands out of theirs and tuck them under my armpits.

"Why aren't you happy?" Mother takes her now free hand and strokes my back.

I bite my tongue and close my eyes. Everything in me wants to scream but my brain is telling me to be strong. I shake my head trying to diffuse some of my inward war.

"Salome, honey, we are here for you." Dad squeezes my shoulder into his side. I hear a crack whistle in the dam behind my eyes and I know tears are soon on their way. *"We need reinforcements!"* Commander Brain demands.

"And we're so proud of you, Salome," Mom adds. This catches me off guard and I'm able to shut my brain out for a moment to look at her. "You've been so strong since it happened." I know what *it* is she was referring to (the death of her son). "You've been like a new person. You've shown wisdom and age beyond your years. And the way you've been helping me in the house."

"And me in the shop," Dad interjects.

"It has been so nice," Mom finishes.

I take in deep breaths. I have to look away from them to think. I don't want to listen to my brain, but he is my brain after all. *He must know something.*

"Why is it you guys think I've been okay with Simeon dying?" The heat rushes to my face in an instant. I know all the anger is coming—all the fury that has been hiding away for the last three weeks. I knew it wouldn't disappear from me. It was right there waiting for this moment. And just like that it is all coming out on my bewildered-looking parents.

"It's because I thought I had no other option but *to be* okay with it. I listened to that stupid woman next door tell me I had two choices. I could either be like her, all Beth-depressed for the rest of my life, or I could be like Simeon and spread the joy despite hopelessness. And I thought at the time that there was no other option, that there really was only death and just death. Death was death and death was it; it was final and there's nothing we could do about it. So I thought I'd have to be stupid to be like Beth and wander around all sad when there's nothing I can do to bring back the dead, to change the past. But I was wrong!"

I stand up from my cot and turn to face my parents. "Jesus of Nazareth has been raising people from the dead like it's nobody's business! Why do I have to pretend to be satisfied with Simeon's death when Jesus could very well come here and bring him back to life? Why do *I* have to pretend to be content with him in a grave when he doesn't have to be? God is a joke! God just runs around with his so-called *Son* bringing whoever he wants to back to life. And he just leaves the rest of us to suck it up."

I turn my eyes to the ceiling now. "Well, I say forget you, God. Forget you and your Messiah. You can choose who gets to suffer and who gets their brothers back so I get to choose if I want to worship you or not!" And with that I turn on my heel and stomp down the ladder into the shop. I crash into a table on my way to the door and a couple of pots shatter on the floor. I don't bother to stop. I go straight out the front door, give Beth the nastiest glare I can manage and take off running down the street.

Chapter Fourteen

Come to find out Commander Brain didn't want to lock my heart up forever. I'm catching on to his tactics. I think he unlocks my heart only after he feels he's successfully crushed it. He probably thinks after so many beatings my heart will eventually stay put, that it won't have enough strength to crawl from his prison even after its been set free. My brain is always pleased with himself for all he accomplishes while the heart is locked away. Seeing it no longer as a threat, he once again releases my heart to me.

Stronger than what either of us (me and my brain) could have expected, my heart stumbles back into my chest and starts to comfort me. I'm always surprised by this. After all the times I've ignored it and shoved a cloth in its metaphorical mouth, it still always chooses to comfort *me*.

Don't you worry, Salome, it says. *This pain is only temporary. We'll be okay again soon.*

I shake my head, ashamed at myself.

I sit with my back against a tree in the valley behind Josiah's house. I'm not sure why my feet took me here but now that I'm actually looking at it, I'm really grateful to my bare feet.

The sight is stunning. It is a beautiful spring day. The sun is shining and the birds are singing. Gentle breezes move the long bits of grass against my toes. I see all the grandeur of the day and wonder how it is I can feel so stormy inside. A single gray rain cloud is probably hovering over my pathetic head.

You're so immature. I replay what I must have looked like to my parents as I screamed at the ceiling and the invisible God there above it.

I've blown it. All that wisdom and age talk from my mom and I've blown it. All the respect I've gained from my dad by working in his pottery shop with him and there I went and broke who knows how many of them when I stormed out. Why can't you just be what your name implies, Salome? Why can't you just be peaceful?

My heart rubs against my ribcage as if it is trying to hug me from the inside. I half smile at it.

I gaze back over the valley and find myself reliving moments with Josiah there. I see us walking together, closer than casual friends would, up the hill, laughing together. Then I hear a twig snap behind me. My head jerks around the tree.

Bethany.

Not depressed-next-door-Beth. It is Josiah's sister, Bethany. *Could I have asked for worse company?* Bitter me resides again as I turn away from her to gaze back over the valley, the valley that now seems like less of an oasis.

"Shalom, Salome," her gentle voice drifts on the breeze to me. I refuse to respond or move. Maybe if I stay still enough she'll find me awkward enough to leave.

Nope, she's sitting down, leaning against the side of the tree with me. "What are you doing out here?" She draws her knees to her chest and sets her head on them so it's facing me like she's ready for me tell her a bedtime story.

Her posture is enough to annoy me, so her beauty only infuriates me further. Her hair is always perfectly brushed and looks like she's just washed it. Her complexion is flawless and her small pointy nose is always blushed. She has rose petal lips and a small frame. She is a female Josiah: perfect with an extra bonus of a hide and seek surprise smile.

"I'm sitting here. What does it look like?" I huff.

Bethany draws her head up from her knees. I guess she realizes then I'm not in the story-telling mood.

"I'm sorry. I guess you must want to be alone." She pushes herself up off the ground and dusts off her backside. As she turns to go I glance up at her face which looks too pitiful to be rude to.

"You can stay," I hear my voice say.

Bethany stands for a moment looking at me. "Josiah won't be back today, you know?"

I'm embarrassed and angry at the same time. "Well, who said I'm here to see him?"

Bethany half smiles then plops down in the same spot beside me. This time she sits Indian style and smiles at the view before her.

"So what are you doing here then?" she asks. *Again!*

"I already told you, I'm just sitting here." I huff *again*.

Bethany leans back against the tree; crossing her arms she purses her lips. "Josiah says you're so nice to talk to but I don't see how."

Offended, I turn to look at her. "Maybe I only like talking to certain people, *Bethany*."

Bethany sets her jaw. I'm surprised she isn't crying yet. Instead she looks kind of . . . dare I say it . . . intimidating.

"Well maybe you should work on that, *Salome,* and you might have more than one friend." She cocks an eyebrow.

I was wrong about the brother. Maybe I'm wrong about the sister too?

I like this view of Bethany. A half smile appears on my face. Maybe joking with her would be like joking with Josiah. I try it out. "Are you volunteering as friend number two?"

She remains firm but a smile is in her eyes, I can tell. "I'll volunteer the day you say something nice to me." She turns her head back to the valley in a preppy manner.

There is no way I'm going to be out-done in the sass business. I know no one else who speaks their mind as boldly as I do and now Bethany, of all people, is threatening that position. I have to act quickly with extremely bold moves. "I like your brother. Does that count as saying something nice to you?" I spout then turn my own head nonchalantly toward the valley while she jerks her head back around to face me.

"Does he know that?" She quickly jumps into her girly voice. I begin to doubt her ability to be sassy like I am but she's made it this far in a conversation with me so I'm going to entertain her.

"Well, if he doesn't, then he's more stupid than I thought." I stretch my legs out before me.

Bethany laughs, "He's pretty stupid, Salome. I'd say if you haven't said it just like that to him, then he probably doesn't know."

"He knows," I assure her (and kind of myself too).

"Well I'll be, if that isn't the bee's knees," she slaps her own knee smiling.

I smile too.

We're quiet for a minute, each of us just smiling with our own thoughts. Then she turns to me, "I guess that means we'll *have* to be friends."

I turn to look at her. "If one day you could be my sister, that is," she smiles broadly. I can't help but feel joy inside. A smile spreads across my face too.

For a minute, I forget what brought me here. I almost start to think I actually am here waiting for Josiah. But then the weight of the past few hours comes upon my shoulders. It brings with it pounds of shame. My shoulders slouch and I stare at a single blade of grass by my feet.

Bethany nudges my side: "Hey, what's with the sudden gloom?"

A familiar feeling comes to me. Like the day at the wall with Beth, I find that I just have to let out of my system all that I want to say.

"I just blew up on my parents, Bethany. That's why I'm here. I had to get out of the house and now I feel bad."

Bethany nods her head while I talk. She squints her eyes together like she's thinking really hard. But she doesn't say anything. She just looks at me like I should continue talking. She's a lot like Josiah.

"Well that's it," I tell her so she'll stop looking at me like that.

Bethany sits up a little straighter. "Why did you blow up?"

I shake my head because now I'm not sure if I want to talk about it anymore. There are too many emotions in me. One second I feel happy with Bethany, the next I feel annoyed. One moment I'm angry and the next I'm wanting to spill my guts. I don't know what is going on inside of me. I start to feel guilty. I probably blew up on my parents because my emotions are so out of control and the reasons I thought I had probably don't even make any sense. *Why was I angry again?*

Bethany interrupts my thoughts. "Here you go again being difficult to talk to. Just spill, Salome. You'll feel better if you do."

I spout off before I think, "I don't know how to explain myself, *Bethany.*"

Bethany looks at me like she could smack me in the face right there. I feel the intimidation again and wonder if she actually *will* smack me.

"Salome, don't make this difficult. You were at home. Your parents were there. They said something to you and you said something back. Now *what* was it?"

Is it just me or is she nosey? I suddenly don't care if Bethany smacks me in the face. I'm tired of her smug looks and crazy attitude that don't match the Bethany I know that hides behind her brother in the presence of Simeon. I've had enough of her.

"I don't have to tell you anything. Who do you think you are anyway? Do you honestly think we're friends just like that? You think just because I like your brother I'm going to pretend to be nice to you?"

I stand up in a huff. Bethany still has a hard expression on her face. "Stop looking at me like that! What is your problem? Are you honestly upset because I don't want to talk about personal information with you? This is the first time we've talked!" I throw my hands into the air.

Bethany is up and in my visage before I have time to take a step back. I brace myself for a smack in the face. Bethany raises her hands then wraps them around my shoulders. She draws me into her and holds me in a hug.

I'm too stunned to have my body respond right away. Bethany's chin tucks over my shoulder and her arms squeeze me tighter. Seconds pass like this with my arms pinned to my sides. I wonder if Bethany is ever going to let go. So slowly, I bend my elbows so my arms wrap around Bethany's tiny waist. Bethany's hand begins to pat up and down on my shoulder blade. I realize then that she's comforting me.

We stand in this embrace for minutes. Bethany only moves her hand, patting my shoulder. I never move. I am frozen with disbelief and still an inward battle rages inside me. Commander Brain is scolding me, insisting I don't cry again. My heart is tapping his shoulder. *"If you please, Commander Brain, I would really love a word with the dear girl. I find that it would be beneficial for her to let her just be her for now. If she feels like crying, so be it. If she feels like talking, let her talk . . ."* *"Shut up!"* Commander Brain cuts my heart off. I feel sorry for the poor thing. *You know what, Commander,* I think, *I'd really just like some silence please.*

So I stand in silence, trying not to think, during this hug with Bethany.

From the corner of my ear I hear her muffled voice, "I'm sorry about Simeon." A chill pierces through my skin at the mention of his name.

Still patting my back she says, "I wanted to come tell you I was sorry that very first week but," Bethany pulls out of the hug and looks at my face, "but we weren't friends so I didn't think you'd want to see me."

I turn my eyes to the grass again because (once again) I feel bad. "You don't have to tell me anything," she says. "I figure it's probably about him and I just got lost wanting to hear about him rather than thinking about your feelings, Salome. I'm sorry."

Wanting to hear about him? My eyes study Bethany's face again. It all clicks then. "You liked him, didn't you?"

Bethany's cheeks turn pink in their centers but she doesn't look away from me in shame (a characteristic I appreciate a great deal).

"I did. I thought he was the most wonderful man God could have possibly ever created. And to think he put him right here in Jerusalem where I am . . ." Bethany's eyes glaze over in a daydream sort of way. I let her stare off into the distance for a moment. I know she is probably reliving some of her moments in my brother's presence, studying his face. I don't want to interrupt that.

Bethany resets her eyes on mine. "If I was you, I'd probably blow up into a million pieces. I know my heart has already broken into a hundred."

My tears are hot and ready to emerge. A lemon the size of Galilee is stuck in my throat. All I can do is nod my head.

Bethany takes her two hands and grabs my arms. "Forgive me?"

After all the yelling I've just unleashed, after all the ways I have screwed up this day for more than one person, I am the one hearing "*forgive me?*" I've had enough of my foolishness. How many times would I have to be brought back to reality by the presence of someone I've so misjudged and yet is so much better than me?

"Bethany, don't be sorry for anything. You didn't do anything wrong. I've just . . ." I search for the right word. "I've been sour." Yes that is a good word to describe me. "I haven't been treating people nice. I've been all puckered up and anyone who gets around me gets all puckered up too. I'm all kinds of sensitive. The slightest thing sets me off it seems. And I was doing so well for a little bit there. I mean, peace. I was *feeling* peaceful. I felt good. But I couldn't hold onto it for very long before I was all *me* again. They should have named me something meaning moody or irritable or something. I'm like the modern day Naomi. Just start calling me Mara."

I could continue on my rant (it was just starting to get good), but Bethany stops me with her burst of laughter (a laugh, if you'll recall, that could pass for a yelping hyena).

"What's so funny?"

Bethany is hardly able to talk she is laughing so much. "You," she slaps her knee. "Oh, Salome!" Bethany finally straightens up. "You're way too hard on yourself."

"I'm serious, Bethany. You've seen how I treat people. Don't you remember when I called Josiah a mud-head? Have you ever noticed that I don't have any friends, that my brother was the only one who liked me?"

Bethany laughs again at me. "Salome, you talk about peace like it's something you have to snatch out of the wind. You can't *steal* peace and hold it captive in you. You can't pretend it's something that suddenly belongs to you. Peace is in you, Salome. Peaceful is who you are when you choose to become it. Stop looking around thinking you're going to snatch some peace out of the air one day. Everyone's born with some peace. Some people just live listening to it."

Dumbfounded: the feeling you have when someone who was recently no one figures you out in record time.

Right at this moment I declare Bethany is my friend. She already knows me too well and still she's decided to hug me instead of smack me. I want her in my life as much as I want Josiah. So I spill.

I tell her everything I heard from Roberta. I tell her about Josiah's story with the boy rising to life and how all that information put together made me blow up on my parents, made me blow up on God. Then to my great surprise, when I thought at that point—the blaspheming of God point—Bethany would surely scold me, she simply says, "I blew up on God too."

She goes on to explain everything.

Her love for my brother seems to have driven her mad. She says when she first saw Josiah come home that night, covered in her true love's blood, she wailed and ripped her clothes and practically bathed in ashes for the next two weeks. She says she was so inconsolable her parents locked the loft and the shop so she couldn't run away. A few times they sat on her arms because she tried to scratch away her skin to ease the pain.

"One day I was so worn out from fighting myself I had to lie down in a cold wet rag bath. That's when Josiah finally gave me the talk I needed. He told me what Simeon had told him one time. He told me the story of the Exodus and Moses. Told me Simeon had explained to him one time that God has a kind of pattern in the way he works. He said bad things usually come before good things so that good things *can* come. He said without the bad things, we wouldn't know we ever had any good things. I guess he knew I had to hear the words were from Simeon for it to make any difference to me."

Completely blown away that the same things Simeon had once said to me that changed my life were the same words said to change not only Josiah's but Bethany's too, I just have to rest in silence. Bethany sits with me against the tree for another hour before she points out it is approaching dusk. Reluctantly, I acknowledge I need to face my parents again. Bethany and I hug for another minute. Then I walk home alone.

I get home to find Mom and Dad are still up. They're staring at me when I poke my head through the floor on the loft ladder. They sit holding each other's hands on my cot. They look like they've worried themselves sick.

The weight of guilt I feel for putting them through today is so much I can't move another step. I stand at the loft's opening, my eyes to the ground.

"I'm sorry," I whisper.

Mom bursts into tears and Dad jumps off the cot to embrace me. We don't say anything else. We just hug for what feels like hours before we fall asleep strung out all over the loft.

Chapter Fifteen

I t is high time I get my butt in gear. There isn't any more time for pity parties. The spring celebration of Passover is about to begin. Today signals the start of *The Purging*. Mom and I will spend the next bit of every minute for this week cleaning every speck of the house. As tradition requires, we'll have to remove all the yeast from the house. Anything that came in contact with yeast this past year will have to be covered until Passover is over. I'm not sure why Mom only leaves a week for us to clean for Passover. Some families clean for weeks. I think Mom just likes the rush of it. I think it makes the days of enforced rest thereafter more enjoyable for her as well. So, I accept the task at hand, knowing full well it is going to mean I won't get to see Josiah and Bethany much this week, if at all.

But time with Mom turns out to be a good thing. We stick our heads out from the corners of the walls we are washing to chat. While we cover all areas of the house, we seem to cover all areas of conversation as well. Of course, we start with the most difficult subject—blaming God for our problems and how Jesus is indeed a good man and how death is part of life and on and on . . . to the more enjoyable subjects which include a careful analysis of the color of Josiah's eyes and the way his hair flicks up in the front because of his cowlick . . . and on and on and on.

It doesn't bother me to talk about Josiah so personally anymore. I figure I have already showed the most vulnerable parts of myself with the exposure of my displeasure toward *Yahweh* anyway. Now all of my insides are fair game. I don't even hesitate to continue the conversation about the sound of Josiah's voice when we start cleaning the shop with Dad perched on his stool. He fidgets around like he is uncomfortable but Mom and I only laugh.

I think Dad is extremely relieved when the week comes to a close and Mom proudly announces, "There isn't a speck of *chametz* to be found in this home! Pass over our home, *Lord Yahweh!*"

After a week of Dad practically being by himself, he is ecstatic to finally do his part in the Passover celebration. It is his job every year to get the lamb that will be sacrificed on Passover Day. For the past 14 years he's gone to the same person—Andrew, the son of farmer Philip (the husband of Naomi who has all the annoying free range chickens flapping all over the streets of this town). Andrew lives near the city gate on the other side of the Garden of Gethsemane. His front yard has the beautiful view of the Garden while his back yard spreads out over the hills that finally escape the city landscape. There he has a herd of sheep which stay on rotation just like Josiah's. However, at this time of year, the entire herd is brought back to the enclosed lot behind his house. There, hundreds of customers (city dwellers like myself) come to Andrew's to get their yearly lamb.

Usually, Simeon and Dad would go by themselves while Mom and I soak our feet, but we know this year will be different. Fully prepared once again, I'm not even startled when Dad jumps on my cot in early morning.

"Wakey wakey, my little pot of sunshine." He tries to tickle my sides but as gentle as my father is it feels more like a massage. I just push him away from me and, unbelievably, I slide my feet into my sandals.

Mom, Dad and I walk through the city holding our little length of rope. Town is buzzing like usual. *Does Jerusalem ever sleep?* I see Roberta is chomping her jaw at innocent bystanders. Ahead Beth and Eli are walking with their own piece of rope. They walk a foot apart from each other. Both of them look at the ground. Chickens flap their way across the street, roosters chase the hens. To my left, a man stands on a ladder hammering at a crooked door frame while a woman watches beneath him. To my right, two little girls stick their tongues out at two young boys who then take off chasing after the girls, cutting across my path. It is this much chaos all the way to the city gate where at last the crowd starts to clear a little so you feel you can breathe your own air. But then of course the smell of manure comes and you aren't so grateful for your own lungfuls.

The lane to Andrew's home is outlined by palm trees. Some of them bow so much they nearly make a canopy overhead. It's as though you are entering a tunnel of foliage and almost immediately the sound of Jerusalem is disappearing behind you. I wish Mom and Dad had lived in Bethany longer so I could at least remember a life similar to this—a life without swarms of people all the time, and a plague amount of dust kicked up by the sandals of Roman soldiers.

Andrew's lane is freshly worn. I can tell he's had many customers through the week. Indeed, some customers are there before us. A little girl only a few feet tall stands, one hand clutching the robe of her mother. She tugs at it persistently until the mother finally swats at her hand. "What, Patricia? What is it?"

"Moms," little Patricia continues. The mother wipes at her brow, her hand shaking. The woman is too skinny. She is no bigger than I am. The bones in her cheeks poke out and her eyes are sunken in her skull with white circles of skin surrounding them. Looking like she is going to cry she quickly drops to one knee and pulls her daughter's hand off her robe. "What? What do you want?"

Patricia's little bottom lip puckers out and quivers. Large tears catch on top of her chubby cheeks. "Holds me," she pleads in her baby voice. She can't be more than two years old.

I try not to stare at them as we walk by. Andrew nods at my father to go ahead in the lot while he continues to talk with the father of baby Patricia.

While Mom and Dad venture away from me, checking over each lamb, I loiter near the fence so I can hear more from this little girl. She is too cute for me to ignore and the mother fancies my curiosity as well.

"No, Pat. Mommy is too tired. We have to carry home a lamb today. I can't be carrying you all the time." The mother stands back up pinching the brim of her nose with her quivering hand. Patricia starts to cry. Her bottom lip sucks in and out with each wail. Her father glances back over his shoulder toward her. Knowing that was her warning to keep the kid quiet, less her husband be ashamed of her for making him look like a fool, Patricia's mother scoops her up and instantly Patricia stops crying.

Though the mother looks annoyed beyond all belief, Patricia nuzzles her head under her mother's chin, smiling. Her chubby little fingers straighten out the hem of her mother's *tzniut*. "Moms, whys do we have to gets a baby lambs?"

Without hesitation, her mother remarks rather roughly: "Because we have to kill it."

Patricia reacts just as I do. We both straighten up as tall as we can, our eyes wide open. I am shocked with this mother's approach while Patricia just seems to be completely horrified. "Kills it? Whys we got to kills it, Moms?"

"Because we've done bad things this year, Patricia, haven't we?" The mother seems hysterical. "You've broken rules, haven't you? You've gotten into trouble this year, right? You've made Moms and Dad mad, haven't you? Well, we have to pay for those bad things somehow, now don't we, Patricia?" Her mother shakes uncontrollably now. Patricia's bottom lip puckers out and begins to quiver again. I want to snatch her out of her mother's arms and hold her. *What is wrong with this lady?*

"Don't." The mother starts bouncing Patricia in her arms. "Don't start crying again, Patricia. Dad will not be happy if you start crying again. Now just you be quiet." Both of them look as though they are about to burst open with tears at any moment. Little Patricia buries her face in her mother's headdress. Her mother bites on her bottom lip and uses her free shoulder to wipe away some get-away tears. She keeps her eyes locked on her husband. Finally, I hear Andrew say his goodbyes to the father. Patricia and her parents are walking down the lane with a new lamb in a matter of seconds.

I stand frozen by the fence trying to take in what I'd just seen. *How could a mother be so brutal with her child? Just a little baby . . .*

"Shalom, Salome." Andrew interrupts my thoughts as he walks past me toward my parents. I nod. I can't concentrate on anything other than that mother's words. I find them so disturbing. I keep replaying them in my mind over and over again. The more I think about it, questions I don't know how to answer start to swirl in my head. *Are we really killing this lamb because of our faults? Why do I have to kill this lamb again? Does the lamb deserve this?* And once again I'm asking the questions I always come back to. Looking at the little innocent lamb before me and imagining his very near future death, I ask myself, *does this make God a bad person?*

The whole way home it is like I'm trying to get out of a maze in my own mind. Each question is a crossroad in the maze. How I decide to answer each one seems to bring me closer to my getaway or further into the hedges of the maze walls. At some point, I just want to stop, plop down in the walkway of the maze, and say I've given up. *I think I could make the little hallway of the maze work for a living space.* I'm sure a lot of people go through life trying to find the concluding answer that brings them into the wide open space of an enjoyable life and never are able to. In fact, I think the people who claim to have found the wide open are liars. They're probably stuck in the middle of the maze like the rest of us, just saying they've found a satisfactory answer so they can live in an illusion of the wide open. I think everyone is probably looking for the answer to life's maze for their whole lives. And that's all that I can conclude for certain. That I'll be wandering through this maze for the rest of my life and the only sure answer I'll be able to give is that I have no idea about the ins and outs of the maze, or how to even direct people safely through it, but I do know there is an end. And thanks to Josiah, I know Simeon is there. He's at the end, in the wide open, where it's easy to breathe. I know the end has to be a good place then. I know it's worth all the confusion of life. I know it is because I'll get to see Simeon there. I know most people would say the end is worth it because you'll get to be with God, but I'm not sure if that's the good news for me right now. Indeed, I think if I saw God face to face right now, we might just enter a staring competition. I wouldn't know what to say to him and after all the blaspheming I've done of him, he probably wouldn't know what to say to me either (besides maybe, "What the hell are you doing here?"). At least when I see him I'll be able to say, "I sacrificed a lamb on my behalf." And with a so-give-me-some-slack kind of smile I'll cross my fingers and hope he'll let me stay there in the wide open with my brother.

With this in mind, I watch the lamb trot in front of us down Andrew's lane. His little black head bobs up and down. I want to give this lamb everything in the world. I want to adorn it with my mother's bracelet, and provide it with a golden bed because I'm just so thankful for the little guy. He's my pass. He's the price I'd have to pay when I finally do reach the end to my maze and the gate keeper says, "Ticket please. You're entering paradise now and that don't come cheap." And I'll remember this little lamb with the white body and black head. I sigh because he doesn't even know what's coming to him.

But neither of us (the lamb and me) is prepared for Roberta. As soon as we enter the city gate, she is calling us over to join her faction. "Matthew, Joan, get over here. I was just about to tell the others the news. You have to hear this too! Come on now. Get over here!" She's out of breath like usual, and yet she pushes the colors of her face to new scales in order to continue talking.

Mom and Dad exchange an exhausted look but knowing they'd be presumed as rude, they tug our little lamb over to the crowd.

She begins by saying, "I was sent to spread the news to as many people as possible," and right then, I know she is full of it. "There is a large group of people making ready for the entry of Jesus of Nazareth. They're waiting outside the city, over the hill there." Roberta points beyond Andrew's house. "They heard he was coming today. They're all waiting over there and said to spread the news that if anyone else wants to welcome him in, they should come join." I can't believe my ears. "So I've been telling everyone I possibly can." A flashback plays through my mind of when I saw Roberta on my way to Andrew's. The way she was running all over the streets talking to every single person makes sense now (not that it is much different from her daily routine).

Dad is all over it. "Which way, Roberta? Over that hill there?"

"Just behind Andrew's lot," Roberta reports, her nose held high.

Instinctively I want to punch her again, but before I can even make eye contact with her, Dad is pushing Mom and me along, practically dragging our little lamb behind us. We are headed back through the city gate toward the hill beyond Andrew's. We are going to see Jesus of Nazareth.

Chapter Sixteen

Once again, things are happening too fast for me to get my head wrapped around them. But sure enough, just over the hill beside Andrew's lot, a crowd is there. The hill forms around the valley like a bowl. Inside, the crowd is dispersed through the entanglement of palm trees. We stop at the top of the hill to take it all in. It's funny we didn't hear any people while we were in Andrew's lot, but now just over the hill, a steady buzz of commotion is wafting our way. Everyone is talking and, though we aren't close enough to hear anything, I know exactly what they are talking about.

A few more people and families scurry by us over the hill. They haven't bothered to stop and stare at the crowd like we are. They must have known this was happening. As they hurry down the hill, the arrangement of the crowd begins to shift forms. From the furthest point I can see, the crowd starts to part like they are making a pathway. People begin to snatch up palm branches off the ground. There in the distance, shadows of men cross over the hillside overlooking the bowl, just as we are across the way. Immediately the crowd breaks into a cheer. It is a cheer so loud it jars my ears and our little lamb starts to tug away from Dad, choking himself on our rope.

Behind the men, a silhouette of a donkey's head comes into view. Then the body. Then the head of a man seated upon it. My heart leaps to my forehead; my breath catches in my throat.

"Come on!" Dad yells like a little kid. He drags our little lamb behind him, who bounds in steps trying to keep up with Dad. Mother and I run behind him down the slope of the hill into the valley.

We stop at the edge of the crowd, our necks stretching with all their might to see over everyone. I jump up and down to catch snap shots of the crowd parting up ahead. Shouts ring through the air. "Hosanna!" "Hail, King of the Jews!" "Jesus of Nazareth, he cometh!" All around, palm branches wave above my head. Some of the leaves smack at my face and leave their little cuts. It doesn't bother me in the slightest. Adrenalin has kicked in. My heart is beating so fast it's like I can hear it humming in my chest. My heartbeat ricochets off my forehead and vibrates down my throat so I doubt I can speak.

Beneath me our lamb bleats. He is probably getting knocked around like I am. I hope he isn't getting stepped on. I take the rope from dad. He looks at me a brief second, then he focuses on the lamb. Then he turns his head back over the crowd. I notice then that the crowd has grown. Behind me another mass of people now stretches over the slope of the hill where we once stood. The crowd must stretch clear to the city gate now. I bet the townspeople have heard the cheers. It has to be echoing out of this valley bowl.

Dad stumbles back onto my foot. Quickly he turns. "Part ways. He's coming! Make a path!" Others shout the same thing and soon half are scooting backwards, the other half are moving in the other direction. I peek over Dad's shoulder in time to see Jesus of Nazareth approaching. But this one second seems to freeze all of time. He's there in front of me, looking totally human, completely normal, and yet he is the most appealing thing in all my life.

Brown, wavy hair sweeps down across his face and nestles on the tops of his shoulders. His bare feet poke out under his tan robe. An earth-colored shawl crosses his shoulder to his hip. He is plain. Just like me. In a poopy shawl and muddy feet. And just like I had imagined the day of the wedding in Cana under the table, his eyes are like fire. Not that they were red, but that they penetrate you and catch something within ablaze. His eyes are brown, just like his crappy shawl, though they were deeper and they are alive. And I know this will sound crazy but they look at me. Not in my general direction, not at my frizzy hair, or *my* poopy shawl, but into my own brown eyes. They meet mine and hold for as long as they can—our whole entire one second of time—the longest, most beautiful second in all the seconds that have ever happened since God said, "Let there be light, and let's give Adam eyeballs."

Then he is gone behind the veil of people again. In between swinging branches, I catch his dark hair. The majority of the time I spend looking at my dad's back. Surprisingly, even that is amusing in its own way. Soon my dad's robe is being jerked off his back by his own hands and with shaking fingers he is throwing it on the road in front of him. I notice then that everyone near the road is doing the same thing. Each robe is being taken off and put in the path. The feet of Jesus' donkey never touch the dirt.

Dad's voice rings in my ears, "Hosanna! Immanuel Jesus! God is with us! Hallelujah!" Never in all my life have I heard my dad raise his voice. He's the most quiet, gentle person you'll ever meet and here he is. I bet if you tried to block his view from Jesus right now you'd get a heavy blow to the temple. He means business, I can tell. He is shouting so loudly his face is red and sweat runs down his forehead. It isn't all sweat though. My dad is crying huge crocodile tears. They run down his face quicker than the Jordan. He probably can't even see Jesus, or the crowd in front of him with all the water coming from his eyes. His voice trembles, "Hosanna," as Jesus passes in front of us.

I turn wondering if Mom is seeing this. But her state of being is more surprising than my fathers. She is huddled down in the crowd on her knees. She is peering under the robes of the crowd in front of her. She is searching through their jumping legs, looking beyond their feet at the path.

Desperation: when your will pulls you to the ground.

I can't take my eyes off her. I realize Jesus is passing by me but I just can't take my eyes away from her. It is pitiful and so romantic I don't know what to do. Part of me wants to hug her and part of me wants to shout for Jesus to stop to see my mother. This part of me is beginning to burn with anger. Here is my mother, the woman who lost her sons *because of Jesus*, down on her knees, getting filthy and stepped on *to see Jesus*.

Is he even worthy of such adoration? How could it be my mother could worship this man when he has taken the lives of three of her sons; and though he could give life back to at least one of them, he hasn't? *What is my mother teaching me? To accept this man in front of me? To love him though he doesn't care to notice you there on the ground trying to glimpse his face?*

I know what Mother will say if I bring up these questions. She'll say something similar to what Simeon told me the night we returned from the wedding in Cana. "Jesus is just one man. It isn't his fault if the rest of the world is filled with corrupt men." And I know rationally that is true. But sometimes it just seems that the Messiah should be powerful enough to defeat all corruption. He is the Son of God after all. He is *the Promised Deliverer, the Savior of Israel.* He's been made into such a high and mighty character and I guess when your name's been blown up to such proportions, it is easy to disappoint people.

And that is what has happened to me. I've been expecting something great for so long, I suppose I'm just disappointed. Then when I start to remember that God doesn't owe me anything, I go and get my hopes all high again hearing about how Jesus raises people from the dead and miracle this and healing that. Then I think it's owed to me. What with the Messiah being so close in proximity to me, it just seems like it wouldn't take much effort on his part to turn my life into total bliss. Yes, I think in a way he kind of does owe it to me. He expects total adoration, complete humility and praise from me. Then I should have a right to expect someone worthy of all that. It's hard to worship someone you don't feel deserves it.

It would be like having Nedra—Levi's donkey—and Nedra never doing a darn thing in her life. She never pulls a cart, never lets anyone ride her from place to place. In fact, Nedra just wanders around as she pleases. She eats here in this pasture, and then goes to that pasture and grazes there, sleeping here. And still at the end of the day Nedra insists she gets called the most beautiful donkey in all the land. She requires fresh daily hay to lie on and if you ever insult her she kicks you right in the gut. So, every day Levi praises his good-for-nothing Nedra. He pets her, strokes her, and tells everyone he knows that she's the greatest donkey that ever lived. He says she can do all things for she's powerful. And all of this is a load of manure! That's what Jesus is to me right now. He's a good-for-nothing, worship-hungry Nedra. The very donkey he's on has proven to be more admirable than him.

With all of this running through my mind, I accept my fate. *Yeah, this lamb isn't going to be big enough to cover my sins this year.*

I was right. The crowd had grown so large it made its way through the city gate and up the streets of Jerusalem so far I can't see where it disperses. It doesn't make much difference though. Jesus is long gone from sight only five feet in front of me. I think Mom and Dad could have wandered through the city after him all day but thankfully, they notice how our little lamb is being beaten to death in the crowd. Reluctantly, we make our way out of the crowd and take some back streets up the hill to our house.

My parents are giddy with delight. The whole walk home they break out in random smiling fits and look like they are going to hug each other to death. I trudge along with the whining lamb, invisible to my parents' eyes. They are so oblivious to me they go straight into the shop without turning around. I'm left to tie up our new friend on the post beside Beth and Eli's yard. While I am at it, I get it some hay Dad got a few days ago in preparation. Then I get one of Dad's old clay pots and fill it with water. I sit down with the water between my legs and watch the lamb lap it up. As I settle down, I hear my name being called.

"Shalom, Salome!" Bethany and Josiah chime at the same time. I am so excited to see them I knock half the pot of water onto my robe, making it look like I have recently wet myself. I don't much care though. I'm up and running to them.

Bethany runs to meet me as well. We collide in a hug. Bethany laughs over my shoulder while I look over hers at her brother. Josiah is smiling from ear to ear, watching Bethany and me. He has a twinkle in his eye like I've never seen before. I have to let go of Bethany and walk toward this star-wonder.

"Long time no see, Salome!" Josiah nods his head, his eyes going from my head to my feet and up again. He seems pleased with what he sees. Knowing it will be inappropriate to embrace him, I stop to stare at him only a foot from his face.

I stare into his big, brown eyes while his continue to trace me. A crooked smile appears on his face. Completely ruining our potentially romantic moment, he says to me, "Your cloak is wet."

I nudge him away from me as he starts to laugh. "It's nice to see you too." I put one hand on my hip and turn to Bethany, who is trying to hold in her laugh (which is a praise).

"Bethany, what are you guys out doing?"

Coughing her laugh out of her throat she answers, "We rushed to this side of the city this morning to see Jesus enter. Unfortunately, we didn't see him. We couldn't get through the crowd quickly enough."

Josiah joins me at my side. I shrug my shoulders. "Well, I saw him."

Both of their mouths drop open like fish plopped up on the shore. "You did?" They chime together again.

I don't want to talk about this but at the same time I've missed seeing these two so much I am willing to make conversation about even this. "Yes, outside the city gate. He rode in on a donkey."

"A donkey?" Josiah cuts in.

"Yes, a donkey."

"Why was he on a donkey?" Bethany wears a face that suggests she is appalled at this news.

"What's wrong with that?"

"Well nothing is wrong with it," Josiah begins.

"But someone like him should ride in on a chariot pulled by white stallions or something," Bethany finishes.

I hadn't thought about this. I guess in a way they are right. Someone who is claiming to be the Messiah should have more of a prince-like quality to him I suppose.

"I wonder why he did that?" Josiah talks more to Bethany than me.

She shrugs her shoulders. "Maybe nobody would give him one?"

"Are you kidding, Bethany? Anybody would have given him their horses and chariots. Did you see that crowd welcoming him in? He could have asked anybody. He's famous."

Bethany rolls her eyes. "Well I don't know, Josiah. Maybe he just didn't want to. What do you think, Salome?"

Both of them look at me like my words will settle the matter. "I don't know. What's it matter?"

"What's it matter?" Bethany puts her hand on her hip. "It matters because he's trying to make a statement. He's telling people he's the Son of God. How many people want to see a god riding on a donkey?"

Using what I think is common logic, I say, "Maybe he's not really the Son of God then."

Bethany freezes like a statue. Josiah drops his eyes to my sandals, the gleam in his eyes fleeting. Seeing his disappointment, I try to recover the situation. "Or maybe he just didn't want to ride anything else."

Bethany seems to relax a little. "Yeah," she drops her hand from her hip. "Yeah, that's more likely than him being a total fraud, Salome."

She stares me down, waiting for me to agree with her. She seems so much older than me suddenly. It appears like she wants to brainwash me. I don't want to give in.

Finally Josiah breaks through the stagnant air. "I'm sure Salome believes the best about Jesus, Bethany. Now," Josiah turns to me in a more perky voice. "We are on our way to the river. Would you like to join us, Salome?"

Smiling partly at the look of defeat on Bethany's face and partly because I like how much Josiah always assumes the best of me, I run upstairs to tell my parents I'm going out.

The walk to the river doesn't seem to take long. In reality, it is quite a distance for just a day of fun. My parents were hesitant at first when I told them where we were going. But I'm sure the longing in my eyes convinced them I needed this as much as they probably wanted to be alone anyway.

When we reach the river, the sun is high overhead. It glistens off the water in a blinding sort of way, and it is hot. Sweat streaks down all of our faces. Though we are red-cheeked, that doesn't stop us from jetting after each other. Bethany pulls at my hair from behind and I chase her down. We collide and giggle then we plot an attack on Josiah. When he isn't watching us, we jump at him from behind making growling noises trying to scare him. He never jumps in fright, just springs after us. We run and scream and jump and laugh more than I have in months.

Once by the river's edge, we plop down in the sandy weeds. Bethany rolls over on her side. "I'm so tired!"

Josiah and I laugh at her as she fights off some bugs swarming around her face. It doesn't take long for her to get fed up with them. "I'm going downstream to that clearing there," she points to a sandy spot free from greenery. Dusting off her bottom, Bethany stomps through the weeds, purposely trying to destroy as many as she can on her trail to the clearing.

To my left, Josiah is sitting with his arms propped on his knees. Josiah's arms are nearly three shades darker than my own. His days in the fields with the sheep are starting to show. He looks like an actual farmer now, not a city dweller anymore. His darker complexion brings out some gold tips that flick at the ends of his dark brown curls, and a hazel tent of green circles his brown eyes.

Noticing I'm studying him, he smiles. "Salome, I've missed you."

His words take my breath away. My cheeks warm with blush but luckily I know the sun has already burnt them.

"I've been meaning to talk to you about something if you don't mind," he continues to smile at me.

Wondering what on earth it can be, I ask, "What is it?"

Josiah continues to smile but his eyes go down to his sandals. I know Josiah well enough now to know that means a few things. One, whatever he was about to talk about he either has to think very carefully for the right words because it is serious; or two, because it is potentially awkward for him. Either way, this means a case of the nerves for me.

"I've been talking to my uncle about making shepherding my trade you know, and well . . . I was wondering how you'd feel about that?"

Josiah picks at a weed and starts pulling it apart in his fingers. "What do you mean? What does my opinion have anything to do with what trade you chose?"

Josiah stops picking at his weed. He chews at his bottom lip nervously. Taking a deep breath in, he brings his eyes back to mine. They are filled with a nervous wonder as if he is risking all he has on what he is about to say.

"Because I hope that one day you might be my wife."

His eyes don't dare move from mine now. We are frozen, just staring at each other. I study his eyes to see if at any moment he'd waver in what he just said. Maybe he'd burst into laughter any second now and say, "Just kidding!" So, I just sit there, unable to know if I should believe what he said or not. But then his deep brown eyes, with the new green lining started to water, becoming bright like the river in front of us. He is serious.

"Oh," I begin. I don't know what I'm going to say but I just know I have to make a sound so Josiah won't start crying on me. "Well," my brain swirls for an answer. What is a girl supposed to say to something like that? Usually we Jewish girls don't get any kind of warning that a guy even likes us, much less plans on marrying us.

This means Josiah is giving me a choice. A choice no Jewish woman ever has. She's chosen. Bought like a dairy cow from her father. She's sold at the right *mohar* into a marriage she isn't prepared for. But not me, not right now. Because of what Josiah just said, he is asking me first, not my father. He is doing the most unheard of thing in all Israel (in the entire world I suspect). This man in front of me is like no other man, none at all, and with this in mind, I have all the confidence in the world now to say exactly what I want.

"I want to be your wife."

The words seem too simple and too short but that is all there is to it. That's all I have to say and that's all I can say before my smile is so uncontrollable it swallows up all my words.

Josiah's eyes immediately brighten with a glow of happiness again, all the nerves fleeing his body. I can tell he wants to grab me up in a tight hug right then and there but disciplined as we are, we just let our smiles consume us. Josiah fidgets on the ground. Together we start to laugh, overcome with happiness. Josiah's laughter grows until he is ripping weeds out by their roots and throwing them in the air like party favors.

Hearing our roaring laughter, Bethany stands on her clearing, "What's going on over there?" she shouts.

Realizing the ruckus we are making, we stop to look at her. Then we giggle together as Bethany just shakes her head at us and plops back down on her spot of the bank.

Josiah clears his throat. Still wearing a smile, he says to me, "So that's why it matters to me if you'd like me being a shepherd."

Totally having forgotten this initial question from earlier, I see it now with more understanding. "If you like shepherding then that is what you should do."

Josiah smiles even more. "I knew you'd say something like that."

"Then why'd you even ask?" I nudge him with my elbow.

"I think I should tell you what will come with this trade, Salome." Josiah still has a smile in his eyes but his face is back to serious business.

"Okay, go on with it then." I tuck my knees into my chest.

"Well first of all, I won't stay in the city with my parents. I'll probably get a tent from my dad and live in it for a long time."

I'm not surprised with his having to leave the city, that part sounded good to me too. The living in a tent part is a little much though.

"You see, there isn't enough land around here for my own herd to be on the same rotation of fields as my uncle's. And then Andrew's herd is on the other side of the city," Josiah waves his hand in the air as if to say "and so on and so on."

"I can't keep working for my uncle as a shepherd. He is just letting me try it out. He has his own sons to think about. They'll have to take up that trade one day too. And so, I basically need to start out on my own somewhere. And when you're a lone shepherd, you don't have your own land *per se*. You just travel a lot. My home will have to be on the go with me."

Understanding now, I nod my head up and down though his words aren't sinking into my heart as quickly as they are my head.

"So, you see if you were to come with me, you wouldn't exactly have an easy life." Josiah has worry in his eyes again as if this information might change my answer about being his wife.

"Sounds good to me," I smile.

Josiah seems stunned. He shakes his head while a smile appears on his face again. "Well that was easy."

How do you act normal after a thing like this? How do you look at a future sister-in-law and pretend like you still see her as a bratty-Bethany? And how do you look at the most handsome man, with dark brown skin, golden-tipped hair, and green-lined eyes, and pretend like he's still a friend of your dead brother when you know he's really going to be your husband—my husband? Let's just stop and take a look at those words. Me. Salome. The angry, bitter, cynical, critical Salome that no one has ever liked. *I* will be married. And *I* will be married to the nicest guy in Jerusalem. He truly is the most adored gentleman in Jerusalem now that my brother is gone. All those bachelorettes who were lined up for Simeon have flocked to Josiah. He is the one everyone wants. He is the son every mother is prodding her daughter toward. He is the son every father is hoping visits him with a trade in mind. Josiah is the one and he has chosen me. So I repeat, *how does anyone act normal after a thing like this?*

I can't tell you how because I'm confident I'm not acting normal. I just can't stop smiling and looking back at him. Praise God above for bugs because Bethany is so occupied with all her new bug bites that she doesn't notice the new me at all.

"Stop smiling, you guys! This isn't funny!" Bethany hops on one leg as she tries to keep moving along with us and scratch one ankle at the same time.

Josiah and I just smile even wider. The walk back home must seem like a torture trail for Bethany, but for us it is too short.

Dusk is upon us when we reach my side of town. Bethany jets inside dad's shop saying she has to ask my mom if she has any herbs for her bites. "I just can't stand it anymore!" she wails as she hurries by my dad who looks up in great curiosity as she rushes by him up the ladder without even a "Shalom."

Noticing Josiah and me at the door, Dad puts down his sculpting knife and wipes his hands off on his apron. "Hello kids," he smiles. The shop is dark but for one candle. He takes it in his hand and heads in our direction. I hold the door open for him as he steps outside where it is brighter.

While he sets the candle down in the window I prepare myself. *You have to look normal. Stop smiling like an idiot, Salome! He's sure to know something is going on and you'll embarrass yourself!*

"How was the river?" Dad turns and smiles at Josiah.

I notice then that Josiah is a good half a foot taller than my dad.

Josiah shares, "It was a beautiful day. Really warm."

"Indeed it was." Dad's eyes sweep over mine then back to Josiah. I exhale. "I'm glad you guys were able to have some fun today. You weren't working in the fields today then, I assume? Did you have the day off?"

"Uncle has all his herds gathered in his lot for the Passover." Dad starts to nod his head like he'd forgotten he already knew that answer. "A lot of people will buy from him this week."

"Yes, we bought our lamb today from Andrew's lot." Dad turns his head toward the lamb who is curled up asleep by the post I tied him to earlier today.

"I also heard you got to see Jesus today." Josiah smiles and starts to fidget with his hands like he's excited for a bedtime story.

Dad perks up too, years of age leaving his face. "We did! Josiah, it was so great; I wish you could have been there." Tears are already brimming at my father's eyes. This is how tender of a man he is. Sometimes his words are so frail you think they'll snap in half by the wind on the way to your ears.

"Tell me everything." Josiah grips his shawl closer to his sides.

"He is beautiful, Josiah. Just a right king, a right king, you could tell. He rode in on a donkey right in front of me." Dad steps to the side as if to show Josiah the whole scene right there. "He was so close I could have touched him. But I didn't," Dad shakes his head. "No I just couldn't." He chuckles as one tear runs down his left cheek. "I was a crying mess, I'll tell you." Dad laughs now as he wipes his left cheek then the right as more tears escape over there. "I couldn't stop crying. You could just tell it was him. Well, I knew it was him from Cana," Dad reminds himself. "He looked exactly the same as he did three years ago."

Josiah pumps up and down on the tips of his toes now. "I remember Simeon telling me all about that day."

Dad shakes his head and smiles at his sandals. "Simeon would have loved this day."

Josiah stops pumping his calves. Dad stares at his sandals. I feel the air thickening, my throat tightening. Looking at my dad, the age starting to return to his face, I feel shameful not having rejoiced with them today when now it is apparent that is what they have missed.

They miss having a child who loves Jesus as much as they do. I am the disappointment in this family.

All the joy that I felt earlier is gone now. Reality has a way of doing that. It lets you forget about him, then comes around when you've lost yourself in bliss and smacks you right across the face.

From inside, I hear Bethany holler up the ladder, "You too! Thanks again, Joan!"

The three of us shuffle on our feet trying to recollect ourselves. Dad sniffles, wipes his nose and then his eyes. Josiah looks at me with a touching smile. I smile but it feels awkward now.

"Hi, Matthew!" Bethany pushes open the door, smiling ear to ear. "Your wife fixed me all up. I had bug bites like you wouldn't believe."

Dad smiles, "Well, I'm glad we could help you out, Bethany."

Bethany looks as though she could jump into an hour-long conversation right then but Josiah jumps in before her. "Well, we better be going, Bethany. It is getting dark out." Josiah turns to face my father. "Thank you for allowing me the pleasure of your daughter's company today. Shalom, Matthew." I watch Josiah bow his head to my dad who has this look of complete wonder on his face now. Dad is watching him like a hawk, studying him to make sure he heard his words right. I know we are replaying the same words in our head, *Thank you for allowing me the pleasure of your daughter's company today."*

My joy has returned! I can't help but chuckle as I watch Bethany push Josiah down away from us. She ruffles his hair as they walk down the street and I see her shaking her head at him as if to say he is the cheesiest brother she knows, a hopeless romantic if ever there was one. Josiah smiles back at me over his shoulder, sparkles in his eyes, his cheeks pink in the middle.

I feel mine blush in return. I watch him till they disappear around the corner five alleys down. I see my dad smiling and nodding his head at me as he turns to go inside. I have to let my body stay there for just a moment longer. I have to freeze this moment so I never forget it: the moment Josiah made it perfectly clear to my father that it is he who wants the company of his daughter. It served as a good warning for my father to prepare himself to lose his daughter to this man's company for the rest of his life.

So, as the fingernail of a moon appears overhead, I tell Simeon all about my day, and how much Dad wished he was there. But mostly, how *I* wished he were there, and I couldn't forget to tell him thank you about a million times.

Chapter Seventeen

T he next morning, I find my smile is still plastered to my face so I run out of the house before Mom and Dad notice. Mom hollers that breakfast is almost done but I say I'll be right back and scoot down the ladder.

Images of Josiah turning back to smile at me flood through my mind as I cut across the street to the edge of Beth and Eli's yard. The lamb is already baaing, trying to get up off his knees to stand.

I hunker down to its level. "Hi, little guy!" I pet him energetically, letting my smile have freedom. I notice the watering pot is empty. I stand, dust off my knees and take the pot into Dad's shop where we have spare buckets of water. To release some of the extra joy I feel in my heart, I start to hum a song of David's.

"Shout for joy to the Lord, all the earth. Worship the Lord with gladness; come before him with joyful songs. Know that the Lord is God. It is he who made us, and we are his; we are his people, the sheep of his pasture."

I picture Josiah in his field with all his sheep. I see how much like God he is. He tenderly cares for all his sheep, like how my dad cares for each of his pots. I see then how much he's like my dad. How he is soft-spoken but most of the things he says means more than what he's actually saying. Dad has to like him. Dad will certainly say yes to Josiah. He'd say yes to Josiah even if the dowry was a single grain of rice.

This makes me wonder how much of a dowry Josiah will offer for me. I stop pouring the water into the pot and sit down on one of dad's benches to think. *How much am I worth to Josiah?* Then I scold myself. *The dowry isn't about how much you're worth, it is just repaying the family back for all I've cost them to raise a wife for a man. Josiah isn't buying me, he's just paying me off, so to speak.*

Still, you can't help but feel like you're being bought. And who would want to marry someone who only offers a little dowry? That would be like saying, "Here, she probably only cost this much to raise, because honestly you didn't raise anything that extravagant." Every girl wants to feel as though her groom would give all the wealth in the world for his bride.

But I wonder how much Josiah can afford. I know he's been saving for a farm of his own one day since the land won't be given to him, so surely that means he hasn't been saving to pay off any dowry. And what if he did offer a large dowry and then he had to save for *years* before he could actually get me?

Part of me can't help but hope with all my heart that he'll ask my father as soon as possible if he could marry me. That would mean I would be his wife that very day. I'd have something to look forward to. I wouldn't have to worry about Mother nagging me, being a burden on my father, having all these guys and girls my age stare at me around town. But another part of me would be sad as well because as soon as Josiah asks, the year of betrothal begins. I wouldn't be able to see Josiah for at least a year before our wedding ceremony. *Could I make it a year without seeing him?*

I try to stop thinking. All these worries are making the joy juice in my brain ooze out. I put the smile back on my face, start humming David's song again and pick up the pot of water to head out of the shop.

"Enter his gates with thanksgiving and his courts with praise; give thanks to him and praise his name. For the Lord is good and his love endures forever; his faithfulness continues through all generations."

I sit the pot of water down and fetch the lamb some more hay. Mother sticks her head out of the upper floor window. "Salome, breakfast is ready! Oh, hello Josiah!"

I drop the beat of hay in my hands. It breaks apart over the lambs back and it bleats at me. I turn around to see if Mother is fooling me or if Josiah is really there.

"Shalom, Joan!" Josiah turns his head toward the window.

I'm completely aghast. I look from Mother to Josiah and back again, trying to remember if I really woke up today or if all has been a dream so far.

I feel the beat of hay roll over on my bare foot. Impulsively I look down and kick it away. Then I see how foolish it'll look if Josiah sees I've covered our lamb in hay so I quickly brush the little guy's back off. He baas away from me to his pot of water.

"We're about to eat breakfast, Josiah. Please do come join us." Mother smiles down as Josiah reaches my side. My heart is thumping out of my chest. Mother's voice sounds like thunder in my ears. I think the whole town could have heard her yelling.

Then Dad's head pokes out of the window above Mom's shoulder. "Well, Josiah, back already?"

Josiah blushes in the center of his cheeks. Today he has on an orange and red striped cloak over his tan robe. A yellow rope fastens around his waist. It makes his shoulder look broad and his waist appear skinny. The bright colors enhance the golden flakes at the tips of his brown curls and highlight the color on top of his cheeks. Seeing how beautiful he looks this early in the morning, I stop to look at myself.

I don't even want to tell you the terrible disgrace I find. As quickly as I look down at my wardrobe, I turn my eyes back up. It takes only a glance to recognize I'm still in the same clothes I wore yesterday. I must have fallen asleep still stuck in my day dreams of Josiah's goodbye smile. And this morning, I haven't taken the time to do anything but rush out the door. I haven't washed my face or brushed my hair; I haven't even put on my sandals again. Mother is going to kill me. She has to be watching me from the window right now, thinking to herself how this is the last straw.

"I couldn't keep myself away, Matthew," Josiah calls back up to my dad. I jump at the sound of his voice.

"Come on up for breakfast then," Dad answers and then pulls Mom out of the window after him.

Josiah turns to face me. I blush all over hoping he doesn't notice I'm still in the same clothes and how disheveled they are from having slept in them. I want him to look at me and not look at me at the same time. He quickly studies me then pulls a piece of hay from my shawl with his left hand. I watch it fall back to his side then notice why his right hand isn't free to do the task. In it he holds his shepherding staff but at the top a knapsack is tied. It isn't large so I know a lot isn't in it, but still I wonder.

"What are you doing here so early?" I tuck a strand of hair behind my ear.

Josiah smiles, "I've come to have breakfast with you, clearly."

I roll my eyes at him and shake my head. "Well I don't remember inviting you."

"Oh," Josiah throws his head back. "So, now I have to be invited by you? Remember your parents *actually like* me, so it's really them I've come to see."

Smiling at each other, I nudge Josiah out of the way with my elbow and head into the shop. Josiah giggles behind me.

Mother is dusting off the extra seat cushion as I climb up the ladder into the loft. She keeps a stack of three extras in case someone visits. Simeon's cushion is still at the other end of the table, but no one sits on it. She throws Josiah's down next to mine on the left hand side of the table. "Josiah, dear, you sit here."

Josiah smiles at me as he takes his last step into the loft. "Thanks again for letting me join you with no notice, Joan."

"Oh, it's no problem at all, Josiah. You are welcome here anytime."

We all sit around the table and bow our heads as Dad blesses the food. When I lift my head, Josiah has his knap sack in his lap. His hands are shaking and his cheeks are pink again.

Usually we all dig in immediately, all hands flying into the same bowls at the same time. This time no one moves. All eyes are on Josiah and Josiah's eyes are on my dad's.

Dad has a blank expression on his face but his eyes do not waver from Josiah's. He looks at him as though he knows Josiah has something to say.

I hear Josiah swallow a big gulp as he looks down at the knapsack in his lap. Then slowly, he starts to pull at the string which binds it together at the top until it is undone. The cloth falls away, opening up on his lap.

The room is so quiet I can hear each one of us breathing. He takes from his lap a goblet and sets it on the table with his shaking right hand.

The silence is broken as Mom knocks against the table in her hurry to get up. She rushes over to the shelves in our kitchen and snatches the bottle of wine. I feel my face beginning to burn with redness. I think I know what is happening but I'm afraid I'm wrong so I don't dare show any emotion. My mouth is so extremely dry I can't find any saliva to swallow.

She sets the wine bottle in the center of the table then knocks against it again as she plops down on her cushion. She folds her legs in under her and grabs her knees. She rocks forward, her eyes boring holes into mine. Typically, I'd probably find it annoying that she's staring at me, staring like she wants a response, but this time I find salvation in her eyes. It's the safest place to look right now.

Josiah gulps again then pulls out a scroll from his lap. His hand still shaking, he reaches in front of me and hands it across the table to my father. A smile appears on my mother's face. She looks like she's 12 again, sitting all Indian style, her shoulders to her ears.

My father licks his lips, then slowly he unravels the scroll. I hear the seal break with a crisp snap.

Everyone is silent. My dad's eyes cross the page in front of him. A strip of my hair that has fallen in front of my mouth moves forward with each exhale and into my nostril with each inhale.

Finally, Dad rolls the scroll back up in to his palm then he holds it in both hands looking at it for a moment. He licks his lips again then puts his hands, along with the scroll, into his lap.

Dad makes eye contact with Josiah but only for a second, then drops his eyes to his hands again. "Josiah," he sighs then lifts his eyes back up with more sternness and confidence this time. "You know you have always been like a son to me." With these words I know exactly what is happening. Mother does too for she shifts in her cushion and she doesn't look at me anymore.

"When Jude and Matthew died, I thought I'd never be able to feel whole again," he reveals as a tear rolls down my mom's cheek. "And then

Simeon came along and the hole started to patch; that son-hole that was in my chest. It was a hole only sons could fill. Years later, Salome came and she gave to me. She didn't have any holes to fill; she just gave my body something. She gave me peace. That's why we named her that." I'd never heard that before. I didn't know I had been so special to my dad. Even though I knew it would probably increase the chances of me crying, I had to look at him.

"Then a few years later, Simeon made this new friend," Dad smiles at Josiah now. From the corner of my eye I see Josiah smile too. "His name was Josiah," my dad nods. "Felt like my boy was always with his new friend or his new friend was always with us. Josiah, you became like my son. You have filled the other part of my son-hole." Tears quiver at the corner of my father's eyes. I hear Josiah sniffle beside me.

"With that being said," Dad places the scroll on the table beside his plate now. "You wouldn't have had to offer me this for my blessing but I gladly accept."

The brightest smile in the world pops open from the boy beside me. My mother's smile opens so wide a faint sigh escapes it. My dad's smile beams but holds a touch of sadness when he looks at me. "Joan, please get my pen." Dad sits a little straighter. Mom knocks the table around some more as she runs across the loft to the curtain of their bedroom. She hustles back with the long feather of a pen and the bottle of black ink.

Dad unravels the scroll again, placing a cup on one end to hold it open. I stare as I watch the black ink form my father's signature. My father is signing Josiah's *ketubbah*. He is signing a wedding contract. *My* wedding contract. My father is signing me over to another man, to Josiah of Jerusalem. That is, if I accept.

If I accept? Am I smoking crazy herbs? Why wouldn't I accept?

Dad nods his head as he pushes the ink and pen away from him. "Pour the wine, Joan."

Mother does so then scoots the goblet along the table, making a scuffing noise. Josiah grabs it then shifts on his cushion to face me. The smile on his face makes one appear on mine as well. And now that I've started smiling, I just can't stop. I even start to giggle, but once I start Josiah can't stop giggling either. He lifts the goblet to his mouth to sip but he keeps giggling into the wine, making bubbles pop up around his nose. He nearly chokes so we all start laughing at the table. Finally, Josiah squeezes his eyes tightly shut, then throws the wine back into his mouth. He finishes swallowing with a great sigh as if it were the greatest thing he's ever tasted. Then, with his hand still shaking, he hands the cup to me.

I don't even hesitate. I snatch the cup out of his hand and have swallowed a big gulp of wine before anyone can even blink their eyes. I have accepted Josiah's proposal. I am now his wife.

It is that easy. It is that simple. It is that fast. In one moment, I am Salome, daughter of Matthew and Joan of Bethlehem. The next moment, I am Salome, wife of Josiah of Jerusalem. One gulp of wine later, I am a new person. And it feels as though that dark crimson juice has transformed all of my insides as it went down. It has filled me with joy, coated my innards with happiness. I just can't help myself; I sit the goblet down on the edge of the table and wrap my arms around Josiah's neck. He hugs me in the tightest embrace I've ever felt. We hug while my parents applaud.

Chapter Eighteen

Josiah has to leave shortly after breakfast. I try to eat as slowly as possible to stretch it out, but eventually I have to eat the last bite. I know him leaving will start our betrothal year (the year without contact so he can adequately prepare our honeymoon). I'm not sure how he'll prepare since he's already warned me we'll be living in a tent. But somehow he has to prepare a place for our wedding ceremony. Technically, I am already his wife, but that wonderful honeymoon night will consecrate this marriage. We will show the world publicly, that I have waited for him and I am his. It will be the proudest day of my life. The second proudest day of my life is this one. I just can't help it. I know my head is held high and I have a bounce in my step. But why try to hide the happiness? I have no shame for what I've become. I would yell it out of our loft window over all of Jerusalem city if I could. Instead, I decide I can tell at least one person.

Beth is hanging up more sheets on one of her clothes lines. Eli looks up from his barrel of water for a moment to see me then puts his head back down to his work. Beth fastens the last pin and wipes her hands on her cloak, "Hello, Salome." Beth's eyes are so kind looking they are mystifying, but she self-consciously bites at her bottom lip. It's not often she has visitors. I'm ashamed to say I don't even talk to her that much even after all she's helped me with.

"Hello, Beth," I say. "I was hoping I could talk to you for a few minutes. I've got some news." Beth stops biting her lip and they spread out to a broad smile like the one I'm wearing on my own face. She shakes her head excitedly then waves her hand for me to follow her as she takes off toward the back yard.

Once she's to the rock wall, she turns to me. Her fingers play tag with each other as she holds her hands up to her chest. "What is it, Salome?"

"Oh, Beth!" I dance a quick circle. "You'll never believe what has already happened to me this morning!"

Beth giggles like a little young girl. "What? What is it?"

I'm able to stop my feet for a moment. "I'm betrothed to Josiah!"

Beth reaches out for my hands. We clasp them together and jump up and down. "That is so great, Salome! You are a wife! That is the most terrific news!" We stop jumping. "And Josiah is such a wonderful gentleman, Salome. He truly is."

I look into Beth's genuine eyes and I know I'm the luckiest girl in the world. "He really is, isn't he, Beth?"

She nods her head up and down. Then tears start to puddle over her eyes and down her cheeks. I'm shocked by them and by impulse I wipe at them. "Why Beth, why are you crying?"

Beth shakes her head with a little laugh. "I'm just so happy for you is all." My heart is so full of love for Beth it could just slowly melt away in my chest. "I've watched you grow up, you know?" she says. "Since you were just a little thing, and here you are, telling me you're going to up and move away one day with a boy."

I shake my head and laugh along with her. "You knew it would happen one day, didn't you Beth?"

Beth wipes her own last few tears, "Yes. Yes I did. Time just goes so fast."

I see the truth in this statement as the wrinkles around Beth's eyes become more pronounced to me. Her white hair seems brighter white today. She even looks shrunken from the time gravity has spent weighing on her. One day, I will be old like this. One day, I'll be the old lady across the street with her husband. Time just doesn't seem real.

Beth sighs one last time and puts her hand on my shoulder. "Thanks for telling me, Salome." I know within these words she's probably thinking of her dead son. I wonder if she would have picked someone like me to have married her boy. By now, he'd probably have a daughter of his own around my age.

Beth—this poor old woman in front of me—she's so beautiful and wise, and for the first time, I realize she's dying.

I could have stayed there in that moment for hours longer, just staring at Beth to make sure I got her face imprinted in my memory, but Dad came barging out the shop door.

"Salome, I hope you're ready to go. Joan, I'm outside," he hollers through the door before it smacks shut again. Then he heads to the lamb to untie it.

I give Beth one last glance then dash inside to slip on my sandals. Mom is coming down the ladder as I try to go up. "Hurry up now, Salome. We have to prepare the Seder meal when we get back."

I nod my head but don't really acknowledge her. I nearly knock her off the ladder as I scurry past. I have excess energy today. I simply can't slow down. I'm so glad Josiah asked me today or else it might be the same miserable day I've always thought it is. I hate seeing the lambs get sacrificed and I don't like going into the temple with such a big crowd either. For years I've tried to avoid this day, but Mother and Father always insist I go. They say it is customary and necessary that I see the sacrifice because it is for the sins of the *family* of which I am a part. But I have joy today because I don't think I'll have to watch the sacrifice and actually be thinking of it in my head. I'll have the sweet thoughts of Josiah in my mind rather than all the reruns of my sins from this year.

I find one sandal under my cot and the other in the stack of laundry by the water bowl. Then I'm down the ladder and skipping down the street to catch up with Mom and Dad. As soon as we're out of our alley, the streets are packed with people and all their murmurs buzz like a swarm of bees. It is such an annoying sound you wish you could swat at their faces. Amongst all of this you can hear the baaing of little lambs everywhere. Some are still tied up. Some are being pulled along like ours is. Others are trying to escape their master's hold and others are curled up by the walls trying to soak up any last bit of sunshine. All of the lambs are going to the same place today. They're going to the temple. They are going to die.

As to be expected, the temple is even busier, but there is less buzzing and more bleating. Lines have formed in front of each altar. We don't line up in the shortest one we see. We line up in the nearest one. Then we wait for what feels like hours as the line scoots forward. Each family is leaving one after the other.

Alas, it is our turn. Dad leads our lamb up to the priest who is taking his hands out of his water bowl. Pink water drips back into it from his fingers. He shakes them then a young boy beside him wipes his hands with the drying cloth. Both of them have expressionless faces. Dad holds out the rope around the lamb's throat to the priest who after a few seconds takes it. Dad steps back down beside my mother.

I take a deep breath, ready to clear my mind now and have beautiful images of this morning sweep in. But now that I'm here, I can't pull my eyes off our little lamb. I've grown attached to the little guy. I've watered and fed him. I've stroked his little back while he's nuzzled up to me to sleep and he's licked my face and rubbed his soft pink nose all over my chin. He's such a precious little fellow. I wish I could rescue him. I could take him home and keep him as a pet. I hate that this always happens to me. I always grow attached to these lambs knowing full well that they're going to die. I always let them into my heart because they're just too cute to say no to. Simeon was the same way (probably even worse than me). He'd always break down and cry on this day. I never would, but it wasn't because I didn't want to. I didn't cry because there are always too many people around. And I've never seen the priest cry. That seems reason enough to me to keep myself pulled together. But Simeon never had a problem with pride and shame. And it worked for him. All the ladies of Jerusalem just admired Simeon, thinking he was one of the only men capable of showing emotion. They thought he was simply adorable. I always knew it was because he showed actual remorse. He wasn't just crying for the little lamb. He was crying over his sinfulness. That was one of the major differences between us. Simeon would think of his sins and he'd cry for the bad he'd done, wishing the sinful part of him didn't exist. I think of my sins and I get angry that I am that person. Simeon was able to put things in past tense. I've always known that it is present tense. I am bad. I was then and I still am.

The priest pulls the lambs head up then slices its throat with his knife. The lamb's last bleat chokes off to a gargle as blood squirts from its throat and seeps from its mouth. Its perfectly white cloak quickly turns from pink to red. The priest is quick and professional. He removes the skin, removes the organs, and without a single bone being broken he lays it on the step before the altar. Then he flicks his fingers against his thumbs so blood sprinkles down on the top of the altar. Putting his hands back into the water bowl, he nods at my father.

Dad wraps the lamb in his patch of leather and ties it up. We're leaving the temple as the priest dries his hands again.

There must be something with the way God made our minds—the way he made us to remember the bad things more than the good things. It seems no matter how hard you try, the images you wish you could forget are the ones that override your favorites. So naturally, Josiah's beautiful face is nowhere to be seen in my mind's eye. No, it is the slicing of the lamb's throat and how the blood which squirted forth from it almost splashed on my feet. And that scene is on replay as I watch the leather wrap bob up and down with each of Dad's steps as we head back to the house. For some reason, baby Patricia comes to mind. I wonder if that little girl was there with her mom today. I hope the mom was gentler today. This is a hard thing to see. I'll never see that lamb again. Not white and whole and baaing anyway.

I see its pink carcass as Mom and I unwrap the leather while Dad starts the fire on the rock pile behind our house. There is nothing but this fire pit in our back yard. There isn't room for anything else. There's only a seven foot gap between the back of our house and the back of the next line of shops on the other side of our alley.

The rocks are lined up in a circle and piled high to form a dome. The lamb has to slow roast on this open fire all afternoon and into the evening. Until then, Mom and I will prepare the rest of the supper, collecting herbs and baking the bread. Dad will watch the fire and rotate the lifeless body. And all of us will think about the lamb all day, not about how good it will taste, but how good its life could have been.

The rest of the afternoon, I help Mom whip up some unleavened bread, crack some nuts and grind some herbs. Eventually I'm dying for a break from the loft and Mom can tell. "Why don't you go see how your father is making out with the lamb?"

I don't even give Mom time to make eye contact with me as she asks. I drop the nut I'm working on and scurry down the ladder. We never use the back door of the shop into the back yard so it screeches like a landslide of slate as I walk out. Dad turns to smile at me as he pokes inside the dome with his stoker. "Hello, Salome. It won't be too long now."

"Hey, Dad." I plop down on some blocks Dad has stacked up beside the fire. "Mom's letting me have a break for a while."

Dad takes his stoker out of the fire and swings it, its tip touching the little patch of grass we have back here. "This day always seems like longest one of the year."

I bob my head in agreement. This whole week has seemed crazy long. It consisted of me seeing Jesus, hating and loving him at the same time, running away, cursing God, befriending Bethany and now getting betrothed. "It has been a crazy week for sure," I find myself saying out loud.

Dad looks up at me. "Indeed it has. At the start of the week you and I were throwing pebbles in the lane and now you're a married woman."

Dad drops his eyes again and sighs, the stoker still swinging. My heart has turned into a puddle of warm water. I can't speak. I'm afraid that liquid will run out of my eyes. So I just sit in silence and Dad stands there swinging his stick, looking like he's trying not to cry either.

After a while, he starts to stoke the fire again and he rotates the lamb. Its little body is charred in some spots. It just looks like a brown piece of meat now. A bit of anger comes in me again. "Wouldn't it be nice if we didn't have to do this anymore?"

Dad doesn't even look at me but immediately he is nodding his head. "Yes, that would be nice." He sighs again and removes his stick. "But there is *some* good news."

"What's that?" I flick an ant away from my thigh as it crawls on the block.

"At least now we don't have to go buy a lamb from Andrew anymore."

"What do you mean?"

"Josiah's *ketubbah*," Dad says matter-of-factly. "We will receive the purest and best lamb from Josiah's flock every year for the rest of our lives."

I'm glad Dad isn't looking at me because I know my mouth is hanging open. This is what Father meant when he said it was too much and that he would have accepted something much less from Josiah when he read the contract. One lamb a year may not sound like much, but for it to be the purest, best lamb of the flock for every year until my parents are dead, that is simply amazing. It's like Josiah is doing them a favor, not just buying me from them. I've never heard of anyone doing this for their *ketubbah*. Josiah loves me. He must really, really want and love me.

Once again, Dad and I are in silence. Slowly, Dad brings his head around to look at me. Then he gently smiles at me. It is a moment when you can't actually describe how you feel on the inside. It is a father-daughter moment. The one where you know you're looking at your dad and you know he's looking at you as if you were a little baby again. Looking at his little baby girl with her chubby cheeks and innocent big eyes that look at their dad like he's the greatest thing in the world. It is that moment that most girls have, and the one I thought I'd never have. It is the moment I realize my dad is the greatest thing in the world and I'm sad I'm going to leave him, yet I know I was made for exactly that. And the saddest part is your dad knows it too.

Chapter Nineteen

I must have lain on my cot for hours, just staring at the ceiling. During the Seder meal, Dad always gives an overview of Moses leading our people out of Egypt. Dad always does a great job at highlighting something new in the story that we may have missed. He always makes us think about it in a new way and reminds us why it is customary to recall it on this day of the sacrifice. And though he's had some really good talks about the Exodus, I still can only think of one talk in particular: the one Simeon gave me all those years ago the day we first saw Jesus.

That was the most meaningful discussion I've probably ever had. All the questions I have about God eventually circle back around to that talk. So despite dad's great point about Moses' and Aaron's relationship tonight, I can't help but only think of Simeon.

The longer I lay, the more I can't sleep. After going through every memory I can think of with Simeon, I am left trying to remember exactly what were my last words to him. I can see all of our final day together in my mind. We've walked Levi to the gate. I've watched Josiah nonchalantly say goodbye to him. I remember seeing Simeon embrace Levi and then I drift off to watch the three men, unknown at the time, but I witness the three murderous, thieving men, enter the gate. And then Levi said goodbye to me and then we were walking. Had I said anything to Simeon during that walk or was I still drifting off in my own thoughts?

I toss and turn in my cot. Surely I had to have said something to him while we were walking. Didn't I? I strain my brain to remember any little thing at all. Had I even said anything to him that morning? I can't remember even doing that. I must have been too caught up in Josiah still. I can't believe myself. I huff out loud and throw my feet over my cot, my sheet to the other side. I look around to Mom and Dad's curtain. I don't sense any movement, so slowly I slide off my cot and down the loft ladder.

Outside, it is completely still and almost quiet. In the distance I can hear something, but I'm not sure what. The sun will be making its way over the hill shortly. I sigh and kick a rock. I haven't been able to sleep all night. I just have to remember what the last words I had with him were. I'll never sleep until I do. I start walking. Now that I've started to think about it, I know I won't be able to stop. It is the stubborn side of my personality.

"Come on, come on," I say out loud. I really want to go to sleep. Why can't I just remember? I think talking out loud will help. "Okay, so you don't think you said anything to him that whole morning while Levi was leaving. Did you say anything to him the night before? The night before I walked Josiah out," I answer myself. "Okay, and why did I do that?" I jump as I see Simeon speaking to me. I stop. What did he say? I walk. He says something to Josiah about how he was glad he came over that day. I can't remember all the words. Then he said, "I'm sorry I can't walk you out. Perhaps you can, Salome?" And that Simeon smile came across his face. "Yes that was it." I confirm out loud. "The last thing he said to me was *'Can I walk Josiah out?'*" I am stunned. Those had to have been the last words we shared. I shake my head because I don't want to accept that. "Surely he said something else when I came back in?" I watch that day in my mind again. I leave Josiah and come up the loft ladder. Did I say goodnight to him? Did he ask me how it went with that mischievous smile of his? But all I can remember is going to bed and not being able to sleep a wink.

I stop walking, ready to face my disappointment. I've found my answer. His last words to me weren't anything special at all. I sigh then look around. My feet have led me to a section of the Roman wall I haven't met before. It comes up to my waist. Just over it the hill of Jerusalem starts to sweep down to the Garden of Gethsemane. The sun is barely starting to crest over the hill. Shortly above the grass you can see the dew rising into the air. The glare of the sun off the mortar buildings makes many of them look yellow and orange.

I turn around to see that I've made my way around the back side of the temple, a place I usually don't visit. I must have taken a left hand turn out of the shop door instead of right. It doesn't matter much. I know where I am. I'm not certain how to get home the way I came but I know I can eventually find my way back. I just hope I can return without the entire town waking up to see I'm still in my bed clothes.

As I head back down the street toward the corner of the temple, I can hear people are already out. And like good Israelites, they're making quite a commotion. I tell you, we are simply no good at being quiet. I wonder for a second if I should try to find another way around this upcoming disturbance but then I think the larger the crowd, the more likely I might actually *not* be seen. Who will pay attention to one lonely walker? So I keep going straight.

But the closer I get to the corner of the temple, the louder and louder it seems it is. How can these people get away with yelling like they are at such an early hour? Does no one in this town mind if they get any sleep? What could possibly be going on?

A normal 16 year-old girl all by herself would probably be scared to approach such a ruckus, but I'm so annoyed with the loudness I'm bound to walk straight up to someone and tell them to shut their face. So I bound around the corner, my fists clenched. I expect to bump into the back of someone as I usually do in this crowded town, but to my surprise, the corner of the temple opens up into a large square there.

I know then exactly where I am. I'm at Pilate's house. Pilate is the prefect of Judea. He is the man in charge of disciplining those who are imprisoned. He is well-respected and highly feared. No one comes to Pilate's court unless they are there to watch a judgment. Today his courtyard is full of people from the front all the way to only five feet short of me. And now that I'm around the corner, the walls of the square form a funnel and I'm at the mouth of it. The noise of the crowd comes booming out at me.

"Crucify him!" the people scream.

They thrust their fists into the air, "Hang him!"

Panic starts to rise in my chest. About thirty yards in front of me the steps of Pilate's house start to climb. At the top between the large white pillars Pilate stands with a man who is so badly beaten he looks like a skinned animal. The man's wrists are tied together with some twine. He has a purple robe on. Blood is seeping through it leaving black puddles all over it. His brown hair is matted in rings of blood and something is on his head. I strain my eyes to see what it is but I can't make it out.

Pilate raises his hands to try to hush the crowd. It takes minutes before they are quiet enough for Pilate to speak and be heard. "Look," he waves his right hand out toward Jesus to display him. "I have had him flogged and still I find no case against this man." Pilate's voice sounds shaky. I've never heard of him to be a nervous man. The way others have talked about him made him seem like he rather enjoyed his job. But today, seeing him for myself, I would say he appears like he really doesn't want to be here at all. He can hardly look at the man beside him. "What more would you have of him?" Pilate asks.

The crowd immediately explodes, "Crucify him!"

Their faces look evil. The crowd shouts with such ferocity, spit is flying from their lips and their faces are bloodshot. Then I notice on the far side of the courtyard toward the steps is a large group of priests. I recognize the priest who performed my family's sacrifice just hours earlier. None of them are shouting. They stand with their arms crossed and they glare at Pilate as if they are trying to hypnotize him. At the front of their pack, the chief priest stands at the base of the steps. He turns his head to one of the priests behind him and whispers something to him. The priest nods his head in agreement then turns to whisper to the man beside him. Soon they all are turning to each other and whispering. They look like a proud group of boys in an elite club. Their matching, flashy uniforms set them apart from the crowd. They hold their noses in the air like they smell better oxygen than everyone else.

I've never liked the Romans, especially the soldiers. But the prejudice between Romans and Jews is no secret. They admit they hate us and we openly proclaim their demise one day by our *Yahweh God*. It is a very open relationship where no one has to pretend to like the other. Relations with the Pharisees, on the other hand, are a totally different and awkward story. The Pharisees claim to be for us. They are our priests, the leaders of our Jewish laws. And yet there is a sense of betrayal there. They parade around town in their fancy robes, they are supposed to be instructing us on how to be better followers of God, but all they really do is say they are the best and won't dare to stoop to other's sinfulness. We're all supposed to like the Pharisees, but I wonder if everyone actually despises them on the inside like I do. Seeing them right now, looking at this beaten man like he deserves to lose every drop of blood, makes me sick to share the same faith they do.

The crowd quiets down again as Pilate raises his hands. "Take him yourselves and crucify him. I find no case against this man!"

Pilate starts to turn to his manservant beside him who holds the bowl of water as the crowd erupts with disagreement. But as quickly as the crowd began to yell it dies down again as Caiaphas, the chief priest, starts to walk up the stairs. Pilate stops to watch him. Caiaphas only goes up three of the twelve steps. There he turns to the crowd and stills them into silence with his eyes. Pilate looks over the crowd surprised that he couldn't get them to be quiet as quickly. Then Caiaphas turns to Pilate. "We Jews have a law," he speaks with a loud demeaning voice, "and according to that law," he points his finger at the beaten man, "he ought to die because he has claimed to be the Son of God!"

My heart stops and my eyes jet over the beaten man to see if it really is true. It can't be Jesus! Please don't be Jesus! My eyes search the man desperate for any clue that it might not really be Jesus. I hope with all my being that it isn't him, that somehow they've seized the wrong man. But how could anyone tell if this was Jesus of Nazareth? This man is beaten beyond comprehension. It looks like at one point he had facial hair and now it has been ripped out. Holes line his flesh and blood spills from them. His hair might have been brown and wavy at one point but now it looks like a sticky black rat's nest.

I try to pull the up the picture of Jesus I have stored in my mind from the day he entered Jerusalem on his donkey. I see it run through my mind again. Jesus is on his brown donkey in his tan cloak and amber shawl. His hair was brown too. It hung in lose waves that swished on his shoulders. And he had looked at me. He looked at me with vibrant brown eyes. They were light brown like a silky walnut shell.

I search the beaten man's face. I just have to see his eyes to know if it is really Jesus or not. His blazing eyes will tell me everything. But he hangs his head like he's too weak to pick it up. I can't see them.

The chief priest's voice rises to a yell and with that the crowd breaks out into a mad frenzy again. Caiaphas and Pilate stare at each other for a moment. It looks like Pilate may be sweating because the early morning sun is starting to glare off his bald head. Caiaphas finally turns like he's won a battle and walks the three steps back down into his faction. With that, Pilate turns to the beaten man and starts talking to him. The crowd overpowers any other noise. They still rant and cheer like they've gone mad. I'm scared now. I can remember only one other time that I've gotten scared in this big city. It was the day Simeon was murdered.

The beaten man barely lifts his head when he responds. I still can't see his whole face. His hair droops down over his eyes so I only see his mouth moving. Pilate speaks to him again then shakes his head when the man responds. Pilate squeezes his temples between his thumb and middle finger then he turns to the crowd with his hands raised again. The crowd quiets down eventually. Caiaphas wears a smirk on his face.

"As custom, I am able to release to you one prisoner." The crowd nods their heads. It is the eve of the Passover celebration. Each year one prisoner is released to demonstrate how Aaron, one of our forefathers who helped lead our people out of Egypt, cast lots on two goats. A lot fell for one goat to be the sacrifice and the other was to be freed. Now with one man standing on trial, he is viewed like one of these goats. It is perfect timing for Pilate to bring up this custom.

Pilate clears his throat. "Who do you want me to release to you, Jesus Barabbas or Jesus who is called the Christ?"

At Pilate's words a man is pushed from the doorway to the right of the beaten man by two guards. The crowd explodes into a roar again but only a steady buzz goes through my ears. My eyes won't even blink. All of me is frozen right here, right now, in this real-life nightmare.

I never thought I'd see him again. The prisoner shuffles his feet forward to stand beside the beaten man. The beaten man they are now calling Jesus, the Christ. Is it really Jesus of Nazareth? And beside him is Barabbas, my brother's murderer.

I try to swallow but there's nothing in my throat but a hollow ball. I think I'm going to pass out. The whole world seems like it's spinning. Slowly, noise starts to come back to me. It's the crowd. They are screaming, "Release Barabbas!"

My neck ultimately starts to break free from the freeze that has captured my body. I slowly start to shake my head, then faster. "No," I whisper. The crowd thrusts their fists into the air, "Give us Barabbas!"

Barabbas is beginning to realize he may actually be freed. He starts to nod his head with the crowd. The dirtiest smile I've ever seen crosses his face. Pilate is looking over the crowd like he can't believe what he's seeing. He must have thought if he offered the worst prisoner he had the crowd would surely change their mind. But now he looks toward his guards like he's made a huge mistake. The guards look unhappy too.

My eyes dance between Jesus of Nazareth and Barabbas. I can't believe I'm thinking this, but I wonder who is the lesser of two evils here. Barabbas killed my brother with his dagger just because he thought Simeon was an un-loyal Jew. He killed him and he didn't even know Simeon. He took away my best friend for his selfish propaganda. Then there's Jesus of Nazareth, the one who claims to be the Son of God. He's been raising people from the dead left and right and yet he's never once cared to help Simeon. He's the son of a God who doesn't love me as much as I thought he did. If he loved me more, he would have told his son to help me. He sees what is going on from up there. He saw Simeon die. He let Barabbas kill him. He could have stopped Barabbas! But something in me doesn't feel right for thinking these things. It feels like I'm lying to myself.

Something inside me snaps. My chest lurches forward from its frozen entanglement. Sobs rake my body. My fingers curl toward my face and I want to scratch out my eyes for crying. "No, no, no," I mutter in disbelief. I shake my head in my hands. What am I supposed to think?

There's no time to think. I look up to see Pilate dipping his hands in his servant's bowl. "I find no guilt in this man. I wash my hands of this. Let his blood be on your hands." Pilate turns, without looking back at Jesus, and immediately disappears into his home. The guards move in front of Barabbas. One starts to unchain the lock around his feet while the other unties his hands. Barabbas is smiling. Jesus still stands with his head looking at his feet.

As the twine around Barabbas' hands starts to loosen, panic rises in my stomach. It is the kind of terror that throws my body into motion. "No!" I shout. Only a few people in front of me turn to look at me. No one else can hear me over their own shouting. "No, this man is a murderer!" I start to run into the crowd. I tug on people's shawls, some of them ripping in my effort to get them to listen to me. I'm so small though. I'm only meeting their shoulders. They're all adults and I'm just a little 16 year-old girl. I can barely even hear my own screams. "He killed my brother! Won't you listen to me? Hear me!" Some people push me back away from them. I merely turn to the next person and start to tug on their cloaks too. They swat me away like a fly. "He'll kill us! He's not a messiah! Barabbas is a killer!" Alas, one swat gets me down. A large man shoves me with one huge hand. "Watch where you're going!" the man yells at me. Then he turns his head back to the stage and thrusts his fist in the air, "Let his blood be on our hands and our *children's* hands!" A woman in front of me steps on my fingers. I quickly try to get up. Flashes of Simeon falling down next to me run through my mind. An image of a dagger protruding from his stomach pops into my mind. I squeeze my eyes shut and use all my energy to push myself up. I'm dizzy. I stumble trying to keep my balance as the world tilts to the left then to the right. From the corner of my eye, I see Barabbas jogging down the steps. Both of his hands are held high in the air in victory. Some people in the crowd greet him like he's a famous person. Most of the others ignore him, their eyes still locked on Jesus of Nazareth.

I lose sight of Barabbas as he enters the crowd. The crowd parts then closes as he passes through. Then I lose sight of any movement at all as the large man who pushed me down steps in front of my view. I have to get home. I have to get out of here.

I push my way through the crowd. I feel lost in a maze of bodies. One by one, people start to step aside as I come through. Finally I make it to the clearing, back to where I started at the mouth of the court yard. As soon as I'm free, I suck in a large breath of air. I squeeze my eyes shut and brace myself, my hands on my knees. When I feel like I've caught my breath, I lift my head up.

Just to my right, the crowd shifts again into an opening and out steps Barabbas. I freeze with my hands squeezing my knees. He takes a few steps out of the crowd, smiling like this is the first time he's ever seen the world. He's dirty. He doesn't look like the clean politician he appeared to be the day he started a riot in town. He wears one messy layer of a cloak. One sleeve is ripped at the shoulder and is hanging down to his elbow. The front is plastered with stains. It's too short of a cloak for him. Red sores wrap around his ankles and wrists where he's been bound. Some of the sores look pussy with infection. He has one large gash over his left eyebrow. His hair is covered in dry blood around it. He looks over Jerusalem as he stops a few feet out of the crowd like I did. Then he turns his head toward me and with a smile on his face he sees me. I feel a warm trickle of my own urine start to flow down my leg. Time stands still for far too long. His eyes dart to my feet as a puddle starts to form there. His smile disappears from his face and he looks confused instead. Then he looks uncomfortable. He licks his lips like he's nervous. He takes one uneasy step like he's not sure where he's going but he wants to move immediately. After a second of hesitation, he changes his course to the right. He walks away from me.

He disappears around a corner into an alley and only then I am able to straighten my posture to stand. My cloak is wet in one spot by my knees. I shuffle my feet out of my urine. Then I turn to see what has happened to Jesus because suddenly I care a great deal. I'm not sure why, but I desperately want to see Pilate out on the stage again saying he doesn't care what the crowd wants and that he's freeing the beaten man. But I turn to see Pilate is not there. In fact, Jesus isn't there anymore either. I just glimpse the top of his head as a soldier pushes him along down the last step into the crowd.

Chapter Twenty

I sprint through the shop door so quickly it smacks against the wall with a loud crack that I was sure would wake Mom and Dad up. My ribs ache and my lungs feel like they are on fire as I bound up the ladder. It bows under my heavy steps and bounces on the loft floor. Dad has the curtain pulled back with one hand as he sits up in bed. Mom is peering over his shoulder, her hair in a tangled mess. They both look surprised but tired.

Sweat drips from my forehead and stings my eyes. I collapse into the curtain, partly on Dad's lap. "What's wrong?!" he gets out before I can speak.

"They've taken Jesus! They set Barabbas free! They're taking Jesus to be crucified!" I spit out hysterically. I'm pulling on Dad's cloak around his throat without even noticing. He grabs my wrists with both of his hands. "Salome, calm down!" Dad looks wide awake now. Mom looks like a fish out of water. "Where have you been? What did you see?" Dad fires his words at me quickly.

I shake my head and try to swallow down the feeling of nausea. I hear Mother say my name. I tell myself I have to pull myself together enough to tell them what is happening. I look up into my dad's eyes and pull him closer to my face. My voice is steady but very quiet. "The people are taking Jesus, the Christ, to be crucified as we speak." Tears clog any more words from coming out my throat. I shake my head again to keep down the puke. "We have to do something," I manage to say, then my fingers uncurl from dad's cloak and my arms flop to my side.

"Okay," Dad pats my shoulder but he's looking at Mom with complete bewilderment. I wonder if he believes me. "Dad," I nearly shout, "I couldn't sleep so I was out walking and I ended up in Pilate's court where this huge crowd was yelling for this man to be crucified because he was breaking Jewish laws saying he was the Son of God and so they said they wanted him to die and Pilate said he would release a prisoner and they chose Barabbas and Pilate walked away and now they're taking Jesus to die and Barabbas saw me and he's in the city now . . ." the words are coming so quick Dad can't follow anymore.

"Salome, calm down!" He holds my face in between his hands and looks me square in the eyes. "I hear you. I understand." He lets go of me and starts to get out of bed. Mom does the same thing.

I jump up from my knees. "We have to go! We have to do something!"

Dad nods his head as he looks around the ground for his sandals. Mom doesn't bother looking for hers. She pushes past my shoulder and heads to the ladder. As she turns to go down it she waves her hand at me, "Come on, Salome."

By the look on her face, I know Mom is as anxious as I am to have something done. We're down the ladder and nearly out the door when Dad yells down at us, "Wait for me one second!" We turn to see his sandals flopping down the ladder. His hair is sticking up every which way. His face looks old today. I turn to look at Mom. She looks like she's ready to run a thousand miles. She nods her head when Dad is down the ladder and all three of us take off running out the shop.

For a while, we run around town like it is a maze. Dad and I follow Mom who is randomly turning down alleys. It feels like we are running in circles. It's like we've lost something we are desperately trying to find. Alas, Mom stops and spins in a circle looking all around her.

I stop to watch her. Her eyes search all around her like a hunter. Dad stops a few feet short of us. "Joan. What. Are We. Running to?" he coughs out through heavy breaths.

I'm surprised at how good of shape Mom appears to be in. Then her eyes stop darting and she stops spinning in her circle. She extends her long arm and points her finger in one quick motion, "There! There, I see them!" She jumps then takes off running again. Dad and I turn to look where she is pointing. Just outside of town the hill of *Golgotha* stands between us and the rising sun. A crowd is making its way up the base of the hill. They're so far away you can't tell how many people there are. But there's only one reason a crowd would be climbing that hill. The Romans call it "The Place of the Skull." It's where they hang their most famous criminals. This is the hill that every traveler will pass on their way into Jerusalem and it's the hill all of the Jews in Jerusalem can see to remind them the Romans are the rulers of this town. That crowd is going to watch a crucifixion and I know just who it's for.

Dad runs after Mom and I follow.

By the time we make it to the base of the hill, the crowd has already disappeared on the top. Fear pushes my adrenaline up to a level I never knew I had. My whole body feels like it's shaking with anxiety. I know my heart hasn't stopped because I can feel it fluttering like a sugar-rushed butterfly. We haven't chosen the easiest path up the hill. I begin my climb by digging my fingers into the base of the hill and pulling myself up. Dirt and rocks break away under my hands and I slide back down. I start again, placing my foot in the crevice of a rock. "Over here," Mom yells before I go any further. She is ten feet away waving for me to follow her. Dad is on her heels as they start running up a narrow path up the hill.

The path twists and winds through a series of rocks. This must not have been the path the crowd took. I think we're further over on the side of the hill. I don't look back or over the edge. I keep my eyes locked on Dad's heels in front of me, watching what steps he takes. Mom stumbles in front of him and he picks her up. Mom takes off running again. I notice the heels of her bare feet have fresh cuts. A small trail of blood starts to lead me.

As we near the top, the noise of the crowd finds me again. I wonder for a brief second why I'm putting myself back in this situation. But something in my gut is telling me I have to do something. I don't know why but I just can't let Jesus die. Who cares if he hasn't met my expectations? If he really is the Messiah, it doesn't matter what kind he is. And how can he ever prove himself to me if he is dead? How can I ever forgive him? How can there ever be a chance of Simeon coming back to life? I still need answers! I still need to see his eyes. Anger begins to fuel me. My pace picks up for the last stretch I need to get up the hill.

I can start to pick out what the crowd is yelling. One voice rings out, "He's saved others! Let's see him save himself!" A sound of laughter and screaming mix above me. Through the crowd a *ping, ping, ping* vibrates down the hill. A man wails with each clank. My mind starts to fill with images of a man hammering another man to a tree. I collapse as a cold sweat breaks out on my cheeks and neck. With each *ping*, the vomit gets closer to the top of my throat. Just as I feel I'm about to pass out, I feel dad's hand wrapping around my upper arm. "Come on, Salome. We're almost there." He pulls me through the dirt a little ways before I can get my feet under me. I don't know how but I'm running up the hill again. The buzzing noise has filled my ears again. I prefer it over the sound of the crowd anyway.

Mom stops at the crest of the hill. Slowly she rises up to stand. Her hair blows in the wind. I hadn't noticed the breeze until now. The wind feels like a storm is coming. Dad stumbles to the top beside Mom and stands up as well. I slow down to a walk. My legs are shaking as they take a few more steps up the hill. Mom and Dad haven't moved. They look like they're staring into a black sky. The sunrise is no more. Thick gray clouds hover in the sky. They look like they're only a hand reach away. I know it's going to start raining soon. Another wisp of wind comes and dries the cold sweat off my cheeks. I'm able to take a deep breath and make my final step to the top of the hill beside my dad.

As I rise to stand, something else is rising at the same time. Thirty or so feet in front of me, a man screams as he is lifted up into the sky. His back is against a wooden cross. His hands are nailed into the cross beam, his feet are placed one on top of the other and nailed through to a half a square that protrudes from his cross. His face is distorted in agony, his body naked except for the covering of his blood, but I still can recognize this man. It is one of Barabbas' minions. It is the thief who took the pomegranate when he entered the gate the day his leader plunged a dagger into my brother's stomach.

"We're too late," Dad whispers.

I pull my eyes from the thief on the cross and look at Dad's face. His eyes are locked on something else. My mom's eyes are locked on it as well. I follow their gaze. Ten feet to the right of the thief, a cross is already upright holding its victim. The beaten man from Pilate's court is nailed through the wrists and ankles. His purple robe is gone. He's naked but it doesn't look like he's wearing any skin either, only blood. This time I'm close enough to tell what is on his head. It is a wreath of thorns. Just above this mocking crown is a sign declaring, "Jesus of Nazareth, King of the Jews."

It is like the whole world has been put on mute in front of me. I can see the crowd yelling and the thief on the cross screaming and to the right of Jesus I can see soldiers are hammering another man to a cross. But no noise meets me. It's like the day in the street when Simeon died. It's like when we entered into another dimension and we were alone before the madness. In this quiet place, I ask God why there are bad things in the world. Why am I here right now? Why is this happening? Why did that have to happen to Simeon? Why is this happening to your son? Don't you love him? Don't you love me?

Then the noise around me comes crashing in like an abrupt wave on a calm ocean. My eyes immediately go to the face of Jesus on the middle cross. He slowly raises his head. His chest arches as he pulls himself up to catch a breath. For the first time, I see his face full on as it lifts to the sky. His eyes search the clouds. Those eyes. Those walnut-brown eyes. They've lost their blaze. His mouth hangs open and his chin wobbles as tears stream down his face. They clear a pink path through his red blood. His chest bounces up and down as he struggles to take in a deep breath. Then he bursts forth, "God! My God! Why have you forsaken me?!" He sobs like a little child but only for a few seconds before he is too out of breath to cry anymore. His head hangs low again. Once more, the crowd starts to yell.

My mom crumbles to her knees and starts to cry, an unashamed loud kind of cry. My dad takes one step forward then shakes until he's brought down on one of his knees. He puts his head in his hand. Shaking it, he starts to cry loud and brazen.

I look to them because I want to ask them if they heard the same thing I did. Did they hear the Messiah of the world question God? Did they hear the Son of God ask why his Father had forsaken him?

I turn my eyes back to Jesus. He helplessly dangles from his cross. He looks little from here. He looks like a weak, innocent, young man. He looks too fragile to ever purposely hurt someone's feelings. He couldn't have known he'd let me down. He couldn't have known how much I hurt from losing my Simeon. Seeing him now, I hope he didn't know it all. I hope he didn't' feel all my disappointment upon his shoulders. They looked so heavy right now. They strain to lift him for breaths. The last thing he needed right now was to feel all of my pain on top of his own.

Some soldiers begin to walk backward with ropes in their hands. The ends of them are attached to the third cross. As they walk, the tree slowly starts to lift off the ground. They go further until the cross thuds down in its hole. The last man screams and spits. "Damn you!" he yells at the soldiers beneath him. His eyes are wild. He looks over the crowd like a crazed maniac. His whole body convulses. "Damn you all!" A mixture of spit and blood spray from his mouth. He is so skinny I can count his every rib. His head looks like the largest part of his body as his black hair frizzes out of control. His face wears so many bruises he looks like he has purple skin. Blood flows from his mouth and down his neck.

"Try to defy the Roman government now!" one soldier yells then spits at him. It doesn't even reach his feet. The soldiers laugh around the base of his cross.

It is the other man who accompanied Barabbas the day they rioted. Only one of them is missing. Barabbas. He should be on that middle cross. He is their leader, the one who claims to be the Messiah for my people and look at who has taken his place.

The gentle body of Jesus hardly moves on the middle cross. The thief to his left is crying, begging for mercy from the crowd beneath him. The one on the right still screams in desperation but his chest lurches even greater now for the breath he needs to yell.

"You!" the third man turns his head toward Jesus. "You claim to be the Son of God! Rescue us then! Rescue *yourself*!"

The crowd cheers in agreement. Jesus slowly lifts his head and looks at the third man. "No!" shouts the first man.

Jesus, the third man and I turn to look at him. "No," he shakes his head. "We deserve this judgment." He looks at the third man, his fellow minion. "We deserve this," he says again as if he's letting it sink into his own brain. "But he," he moves his head like he's trying to motion to Jesus. "He doesn't. He's done nothing wrong." The first man chokes into a cry again. The third man wails in anger but he has no words.

Jesus remains looking at the first man. After a moment the thief snorts in his last set of sobs and leans his head back against his cross, his eyes on Jesus. A single tear rolls down his cheek as they look at each other. The first man takes in a deep breath then leans forward. "Jesus, remember me when you enter your kingdom."

The crowd seems to hush at his words. My parents pull their heads up. Their sobs grow quiet as they, along with every other person on this hilltop, stare at Jesus. He doesn't even move. The crowd leans in to hear what he has to say as his mouth opens. "Today," he nods his head, "truly, you will be with me in paradise."

The first man cries. The third man wails in more anger. The crowd roars with hatred, "Blasphemer!" I slowly get to my knees. I have no more strength to stand. Then the rain starts to fall.

Chapter Twenty - One

I must have sat there for hours before my parents scooped me up under my armpits lifting me to my feet. I had been a frozen zombie just staring at Jesus on the middle cross. I guess I'd wanted to see some beam of light come down from the rain clouds and touch Jesus. Or maybe I just wanted to get all the looking at him in because I knew this was the last time I'd ever see him. But the hill top had become pretty crowded. Caiaphas and his clan had showed up on their horses. They tromped around like they owned the grass. I guess Mom and Dad wanted to leave when they'd shown up. They'd probably also say they were thinking of my health, that we shouldn't be in the rain all that long, or that I shouldn't be staring at nearly dead bodies all that long either.

Once we arrive home, we all just sit in the middle of the loft on Simeon's old blankets. We don't even change our wet clothes. We just wrap blankets around each other and stay numb to the world. The only feeling I can recognize is how much I wish Josiah was here to talk to me. I don't want to go through this alone. I don't even know if he knows what is happening outside. Is he stuck in the rain with his sheep somewhere? Is he watching the hilltop from a distance?

Jerusalem is waking up now. More and more people will be seeing this terrible day—the day our Messiah was crucified by the Romans. This is the day everyone will stop believing in Messiahs and new beginnings, and good things from a good God. This will mark the day of unbelief for the Israelite people.

The whole day has gone by in a creepy kind of quiet. Now that it is midnight, all I can continue to think about is Jesus' cry from the cross, "My God, why have you forsaken me?" God. Jesus cried out to God. That could only mean one thing: Jesus *believed* in God. Even while he was hanging there on a cross, completely helpless, he was still believing in God.

As I sit here on my cot in the middle of the night I twist my fingers in and out of each other thinking about this. Jesus questioned God. He asked him where in the world he was. The man who claimed to be the very Son of God was asking where his dad had gone. This just simply puzzles me. Puzzles me because Jesus had felt the same way I had felt in that moment. All alone.

Yet, Jesus didn't *have* to be there. He didn't have to hang on that cross, did he? Like the soldiers were all shouting, "He saved others, have him save himself." Why didn't angels come down? Why didn't God come down? Why didn't Jesus just climb down all by himself?

Beads of sweat start to form on my head because I'm thinking so hard. My stomach is in extreme pain. I don't remember eating today but it feels like there's soiled food in my stomach. This man Jesus I just don't understand.

"Salome?" Dad's voice makes me jump. Through the darkness I see him coming out from behind his curtain of a room. "Are you still awake?"

I twist my sweaty palms together and sigh. Dad sits on my cot next to me. He pats my back a few times then squeezes my arm into his side. "Salome, you don't have to worry about Barabbas. Nothing is going to happen to you."

Dad's words surprise me. I hadn't even thought about Barabbas since the images of the hilltop had taken over my mind.

I shake my head. "No, it's not that, Dad."

Dad unwraps his arm and brings it back to his lap. "What is it then?"

"I just don't understand why Jesus did that."

Dad nods his head slowly. He swallows then asks me, "Did what?"

My eye brows cross. I look at Dad through the darkness of our loft and wonder if it is really my dad I'm talking to. "Why he died today." I try to say without yelling. "Why he hung on the cross, Dad. Why all of this happened." I raise my hands in the air then let them slap back down on my thighs.

"I see," Dad nods his head.

It is quiet for a while. Just long enough to let my anger get the best of me. "Aren't you asking yourself the same questions?" I shoot at him.

Dad is still for a moment. "I was thinking more along the lines of, 'Why did we do that to Jesus?'"

He doesn't make eye contact with me though I'm boring holes through his head with my eyes. I'm confused and feeling like I've probably had evil thoughts again, hearing how Dad's thoughts are the opposite of mine.

"But you're right," Dad surprises me again. "I don't know why God let this happen."

"And neither did Jesus apparently. That's what I keep thinking about: how Jesus asked 'God why have you forsaken me?' there on the cross today. Even Jesus didn't seem to understand why God was letting this happen to him."

Dad looks at me now though I'm busy watching the reruns of Jesus crying out in pain in my head again.

"That is a very good question." Dad says as though he's just thinking of these things as I've said them to him.

But words are coming out of me before I'm thinking, "But when do we ever understand why God does the things he does? I mean, you didn't understand why God let Matthew and Jude die. We didn't understand why he let Simeon die. I didn't understand why Jesus raised certain people from the dead and not Simeon. Why should this be any different? The thing is, we don't understand God's ways but," thoughts start to form in my head that make me stop and actually process them. I know they can't be my own thoughts because they are too good and pure to be my own. I hear the words of our sacred scroll from the prophet Isaiah rolling through my mind. Without my knowing, they are rolling out of my mouth, "*For my thoughts are not your thoughts, neither are your ways my ways,' declares the Lord. 'As the heavens are higher than the earth so are my ways higher than your ways and my thoughts higher than your thoughts.'"* Another passage comes, *"For who has understood the mind of the Lord or instructed him as his counselor?'"*

I'm quiet as I try to think about what these passages mean and how it was that they came to my mind. Before I can understand any of it, Dad whispers: "That was the wisest, most beautiful thing, Salome."

Dad's words have once again caught me off guard. I turn to look at him because his voice sounds as though he is crying. I search for any tears and can't make out any in the dark.

Finally, Dad straightens his back a little. "You're right." He says. "We don't need to question why God has let these things happen, not when we know that he really is God." Dad breathes like he's inhaling a truth he doesn't want to accept. "And I know Jesus was the Messiah. I truly believe he was the Son of God. And so, I won't question today, Salome. It must have some meaning to God that we don't understand yet." He swallows hard like he's trying to swallow a large, round olive whole. His voice comes back out shaking and his bottom lip quivers. "And I don't know why my sons were all taken from me, but I know it hurt more than anything I've ever experienced in this life." Tears start to fall down my father's cheeks. I'm too stunned to comfort him. "And so I can't be angry at God for what has happened today because I know how he probably feels." He swallows down his tears then looks at me. "He lost his son today the same as I have."

His words hit me like a large boulder careening down a hill. All of me feels shattered. I feel released into a floating atmosphere where I see reality and meaning all around me. I can see everything clearly from all angles. It is large. Its expanse is too far for me to see any ending. And I'm a small bunch of broken pieces floating through one little portion of it. It is here that I know I've communicated with Simeon. I know all my words I've thrown at out at the moon have gone here to this floating atmosphere where it looks like everything could be lost but actually it is where it is found. Simeon found my words here. And it is here I find Simeon's words again. I decide I have to tell my father them.

I collect myself together again and find myself on my cot. Dad is drying his wet face.

I clear my throat so he looks at me. "Dad, one time I asked Simeon if God was a bad person." Dad looks at me like a small child. I suddenly feel like I'm telling a little kid a bed time story. "It was the day Mom told me about Matthew and Jude for the first time. She told me how Herod had made that decree that all the baby boys be killed because he wanted to kill Jesus. And I just thought it wasn't fair that God let his son live when you and Mom's boys had to die." Dad's lip quivers again. His eyes are full of tears but he keeps them locked on mine. "Simeon told me something similar happened to Moses. How he was a baby when Pharaoh decreed all the baby boys be thrown into the Nile. And Simeon told me Moses was saved just like Jesus was, out of everybody. He said Moses was saved so he could free our people from Egypt. A lot of babies died but because God saved one of them, he was able to save a whole bunch of other people later." Dad nods his head like he's understanding.

I swallow and try to remember the point I was going to make. All I can remember is that there is one thing I definitely wanted to say from all this. "Anyway, Simeon told me something that night that has since changed everything for me. It's made me look at a lot of things differently. And I think it is how we should look at this situation." Dad looks at me like he's clinging to every word. I hope they don't let him down. They seem very simple now that I'm about to say them. I take his hand in mine and feel this weight of warmth rest on my back. It seeps down through my skin, through my spine and fills all of my insides. The warmth makes me smile a little. I close my eyes and breathe it all in. It feels like peace. I open my eyes and say with complete confidence, "God has a way of working, Dad. I think something bad usually comes before something good."

I find myself in the same predicament here, trying to end this story, as when I first started to tell it. I couldn't find the right place to start and now I'm not sure if this is the right place to stop. So much more happens. Jesus rises from the dead two days later. I marry the man of my dreams, move to the wilderness in a tent for a while until years later when we finally own our own land and flock. I have three sons and one daughter.

Beth and Eli passed away. My dad passed then my mom, then Josiah's parents. I've never once seen Barabbas. I grow old and happy . . . and did I mention Jesus rose from the dead?

It was the greatest day in history for my people. Sure some people tried to lie and say Jesus' body was stolen from the tomb. Some say he didn't actually die that day on the cross, and all of it was a scam so he could continue to play god. But more of us saw it than could deny it. I was there the day Jesus ascended into heaven. I saw his body lift into the clouds. I saw my Messiah leave this world and promise me he'll be back one day. I know it is all true. And so all that proceeded from that day can be summed up this way: I am Salome of Jerusalem, now the wife of Josiah of Jerusalem. I once was not my name, but now I am me. I am Peace.

www.ingramcontent.com/pod-product-compliance
Lightning Source LLC
Chambersburg PA
CBHW031237260626
47169CB00007B/2337